In this engaging and dynamic collection of essays by ten Black women writers in Britain are personal stories, glimpses of history, discussions of the intentions and obligations of writing itself, a sense of culture and of community in the face of British racism, and a powerful sense of resistance. This is writing that comes from a clear-eyed and determined sense of collectivity, of mutual struggle; its themes are colonialism and slavery, male domination, the family and motherhood, work and sexuality. The contributors – poets, fiction and non-fiction writers, some of whom were born in Britain, others originally from other countries – are: Valerie Bloom, Beverley Bryan, Stella Dadzie and Suzanne Scafe (the latter three writing about their collective work in producing *The Heart of the Race: Black Women's Lives in Britain*), Amryl Johnson, Grace Nichols, Marsha Prescod, Lauretta Ngcobo, Agnes Sam, and Maud Sulter. And in her comprehensive introduction, Lauretta Ngcobo traces the history of Black women's writing in Britain, discussing also the work of other writers – Barbara Burford, Buchi Emecheta and Joan Riley. Poems, prose pieces and critical commentaries combine to offer a view of the rich and multi-faceted cultural tradition of this writing in the 1980s.

Lauretta Ngcobo was born in South Africa. After the 1960s political upheavals, she went into exile with three of her children, eventually settling in London, where she works as a teacher and continues to write. Her novel, *Cross of Gold*, was published in 1981. She is at work on a second novel.

LET IT BE TOLD
Essays by Black Women in Britain

edited by
Lauretta Ngcobo

Published by VIRAGO PRESS Limited 1988
Centro House, 20-23 Mandela Street, London NW1 0HQ

First published by Pluto Press 1987

This collection copyright © Lauretta Ngcobo 1987
Revised introduction copyright © Lauretta Ngcobo 1988
Copyright © individual contributors 1987

British Library Cataloguing in Publication Data

Let it be told: essays by black women writers in Britain.
  1. Women, Black——Great Britain——
  Social life and customs
  I. Ngcobo, Lauretta
  941'00496   DA125.N4

  ISBN 0-86068-633-7

Printed in Great Britain by
Cox & Wyman Ltd, Reading, Berkshire

CONTENTS

ACKNOWLEDGEMENTS

Great acknowledgement is made for permission to reprint the following:

Excerpts from *The Heart of the Race* by Beverley Bryan, Stella Dadzie & Suzanne Scafe. Copyright © Bryan, Dadzie & Scafe, 1985. Reprinted by permission of Virago.

Excerpts from *Long Road to Nowhere* by Amryl Johnson. Copyright © Amryl Johnson, 1985. Reprinted by permission of Virago.

Excerpts from *Touch Mi; Tell Mi!* by Valerie Bloom. Copyright © Valerie Bloom 1983. Reprinted by kind permission of Bogle-L'Ouverture Publications.

Excerpts from *As a Black Woman* by Maud Sulter. Copyright © Maud Sulter 1985. Reprinted by kind permission of Akira Press.

Excerpts from *Cross of Gold* by Lauretta Ngcobo. Copyright © Lauretta Ngcobo 1981. Reprinted by kind permission of Longman Publishers.

Excerpts from *i is a long memoried woman* by Grace Nichols. Copyright © Grace Nichols 1983. Reprinted by kind permission of Karnak House.

Excerpts from *Land of Rope and Tory* by Marsha Prescod. Copyright © Marsha Prescod 1985. Reprinted by kind permission of Akira Press.

EDITOR'S NOTE

Let it be Told is a collection of essays by Blackwomen in Britain, essentially discussing their experiences and their outlook on life as revealed in their writing. Some of them originally came from other countries but now live in Britain. Some write about the British experience and others write from a British perspective about the Black experience worldwide. The structure of the book will not be found to be uniform. Writers were asked to contribute individual chapters, each of which is preceded by a biographical note, and in some cases there is also a short critical appraisal of that author's work.

However, this volume is not intended as a critique, although there is a growing need for such a book. The time for an extensive critical study of Blackwomen's writing in Britain may not yet have come, but the temptation to look at some significant work became too great. Those writers who feature here have not been chosen on merit alone, as against those whose work does not appear or who have not even been published: a book of this nature can encompass only so many and it was not possible to invite as many contributions as I would have liked. Not all the contributors can yet claim publications of their own; but as Blackwomen writers we share a feeling of oneness whether we are published or not, for the publication of anyone's work is fortuitous and we have all felt disillusionment with the British publishing establishment. Among us, unpublished writers can enjoy as much recognition as those published, performing in public and often sharing platforms with published writers.

In my Introduction, which I have revised for the 1988 Virago paperback edition, I have kept criticism of individual writers to a minimum, feeling that their own essays will speak for them. But I have given more attention to the works of a few important writers whose own words are not included in the body of this volume. The contributors represented do not cover the full range of genres in which Blackwomen writers are working. For instance, there are no biographers and no playwrights included, although there are Blackwomen playwrights throughout the country whose works are being increasingly performed in fringe theatres. Published writings by Blackwomen in Britain are still relatively few and far between. We do not apologize for this. Black British society as a viable entity is very young indeed, barely fifty years old if the mid-1950s is taken as the point when Black people began to settle in Britain in significant numbers – although for hundreds of years prior to this there had been pockets of Black communities in various parts of Britain such as Liverpool and Wales.

This book has a historic place to fill in terms of our literary development in Britain. Here we present a sweeping bird's-eye view of what is emerging on the women's literary front in this country. We count ourselves fortunate to be present at the dramatic moment of the creation of a new tradition. A few years ago there was nothing called Black British Art and Culture. Today there is.

We women are not alone in this making of literary history; we are with Blackmen in Britain. The world over, few women have experienced the excitement of being the co-authors of their culture, for few societies have accorded women the status of equality with men, regarding them rather as inferior beings. As a result, culture has been undeniably a male product and preserve, reflecting male values and safeguarding the interests of men. Women are the practitioners of what is dictated to or imposed upon them. Until the advent of feminist thought, women accepted this treatment with little show of rebellion, after centuries of conditioning. We, however, have a unique opportunity in that we can restructure our culture together, men and women co-operating and sharing insights.

The whole canvas of Black culture in Britain is speckled with an ever-growing number of firsts in every field. It cannot be denied that the host society has been more ready to embrace and facilitate publications by Black male writers, who themselves have tended in their initial euphoric acceptance to spare little thought for Blackwomen. But as we experience the birth pangs of this culture together, the gap is narrowed each time one more woman appears in print. What we see as differences between male and female writing may only be a manifestation of diversity in the richness of one Black literature.

What should be obvious to all those who are interested in Black cultural history is that Blackwomen have always been involved in the creation and performance of our literature, especially oral literature. From time immemorial, we have been the undisputed practitioners of the art. Our involvement in this did not begin only when we changed to the scripted form of expression. We have been writing for a long time; it is now that these writings are beginning to come out into the open. So if there is a certain inevitable incompleteness about this book, it is one that is daily altered by our changing position as Blackwomen writers in Britain at this point in history.

It is my pleasure to express my indebtedness to all the women who have contributed towards the success of *Let it be Told*.

Lauretta Ngcobo
London, 1988

INTRODUCTION

In the mainstream of life in Britain today, Blackwomen are caught between white prejudice, class prejudice, male power and the burden of history. Being at the centre of Black life, we are in daily confrontation with various situations and we respond in our writings to our experiences – social, political and economic. We write about life as we live it. We are at a stage when we face the onerous task of creating strong self-images, for the need to confront and change the prevailing perception of us has never been greater. We want to materialize in the heart of this racist and sexist society where Blackwomen are invisible, to replace the stereotypes in which the white world and Blackmen wish to constrict us.

While seeking to alter the misunderstood reality of Black-women, we are in the throes of self-discovery, for decades of conditioning have taken their toll. As a group we suffer the self-perpetuating psychological mutilation of oppression: a battered self-image, which has undermined our confidence; diminished possibilities for self-expression, linked with poor educational opportunities; internalized images of ourselves as depicted by others; and countless self-inflicted wounds. This is what we mean to shake off. We have been caricatured as ignorant drudges, as evil prostitutes, as castrators of men. But this is not how we see ourselves. We know otherwise. We embody a largeness and a continuity far beyond these limiting stereotypes. While reiterating the well-worn bitter reactions to a racist society, we are laying claim to our selfhood, making bold to assert ourselves as women: separate from and equal to men, demanding recognition not only from the host society but from our own community. We write in order to create new models for our young, and a new fortitude. We seek to make people look on us and see a new breed of non-compliant women. We mean to shed the old image of Blackwomen with a dead-end destiny. We are in search of our hidden triumphs that helped us to survive the horrors of the past, triumphs that have gone unheeded before.

Writing as an art differs markedly from our traditional oral forms of communication. Oral tales are inclusive and in a variety of ways reach out to as many people as possible, so that ultimately they become the common property of the majority. Writing, on the other hand, is designed for a select class, those who can read. Essentially, therefore, it is exclusive, intended from the outset to reach only the eyes of those who have achieved literacy: the script itself automatically excludes those who do not have it. The written presentation of even the simplest ideas is often couched in complexities that, albeit unintentionally, exclude many people. This exclusive quality of the written word can be as intimidating to the writer as to the reader. Questions such as "Who am I writing for?" or "How should I put this to this or that audience?" arise, cowing writers into saying less than they wish. These and many other strictures can lead to self-censorship, with the writer being tamed into attempting to please the imagined reader or publisher, more so if the publisher is white and male and the writer Black and female. But the position of our writers demands of them absolute belief in what they say, for they are charged with a responsibility to inform and express, to address themselves to the disadvantage in our communities.

Many Blackwomen writers prefer to communicate through poetry, a medium of expression which effectively enables them to deal immediately with the subjects that engage Black society, and to address our audiences in the languages they understand and appreciate. Some write in the Creole of the Caribbean, the language which arouses more emotion than most, forged as it was in those centuries of darkness, out of scraps of human speech from everywhere. It is the language of triumph and achievement. In some of this poetry, the African tradition rooted in oral art and performance is clear. It creates links between the writer and the rest of the community. Such is the work of Marsha Prescod in her book *Land of Rope and Tory* (1985) and Valerie Bloom in *Touch Mi; Tell Mi* (1983). As

Marsha Prescod has said: "We all come from a tradition of talkers – verbal communicators. I'm a verbal performer and less of a writer." Such literature derives its power not only from the message of the craft but also from the personality of the artist. It depends a great deal on the flair of the performer, and the audience are participants while being informed and entertained. Its "rapping" rhythm involves the listeners emotionally in the performance; the language of the ghetto encourages them to embrace this poetry as their own. In it they see themselves and laugh, for it gives vent to humour as well as to social protest. Valerie Bloom describes her poetry as not only oral but aural. It has a special appeal for the young but is equally absorbing for adults, covering a wide range of subjects from Jamaican village life to burning issues of international concern such as the political developments in the Caribbean, the Middle East, in Africa and in Britain. She writes with a twinkle in her eye, for she can easily find irony in any situation. In a conversational style she explores people's fears and joys and their comic ways out of predicaments. Marsha Prescod, on the other hand, has an eye for the bitter ironies that engulf society in Britain; she is extremely satirical in her treatment of social issues and more than occasionally raises a laugh in her audience.

This outspoken poetry stirs a sense of pride and a spirit of resilience as it probes political questions and engages in self-investigation. It is dramatic. It forces people to listen, young and old. Performed at various gatherings, at political rallies, in churches and in entertainment halls, it captures audiences who would never buy a poetry book or go to a library. It helps them to laugh at their own pain and to pick up new courage to face their arduous lives.

There is a parallel between such poetry and the so-called riots in Brixton, Toxteth, Handsworth and other inner-city areas. Without justifying rioting as a method of communication, it cannot be denied that this is the ultimate weapon in the quest for attention: "Riot is the language of the unheard." The screams in the burning flames of our chaotic neighbourhoods – the effort to be heard from the hidden recesses of Black communities. Burning down a building is a demand for change, for new structures and a new regard. It may be reckless, but so is the disregard of these communities by the authorities. Out of our acrid neighbourhoods also springs this rioting literature. It is not art for art's sake; its vibrancy and immediacy are intended to forge unity and wrench a new identity. We as Black writers at times displease our white readership. Our writing is seldom genteel since it springs from our experiences which in real life have none of the trimmings of gentility. If the truth be told, it cannot titillate the aesthetic palate of many white people, for deep down it is a criticism of their values and their treatment of us throughout history.

Few of our writings are strictly personal in the subjective sense of encompassing individual exploits. Rather, they reflect a collective subject, the common experience of Blackwomen reaching, reflecting and capturing different shades and depths and heights of moods. Amryl Johnson captures them all and wraps them in her volume *Long Road to Nowhere*. We deal with male domination, with racism, colonialism and slavery as they pertain to women, with motherhood and other subjects that highlight a Black female perspective. Grace Nichols in her award-winning book *i is a long memoried woman* (1983) deals in depth with the experience of women under slavery, tracing it through the centuries. Her poem "We the Women" points out how historians have chosen to forget, if not nullify, that experience: we who "cut/ clean fetch dig sing/ yet we the women/ who praises go unsung/ voices go unheard". In "Sugar Cane" she describes this symbol of our enslavement in strangely powerful erotic imagery – "we feel the/ need to strangle/ the life/ out of him". She recalls a time when women would strangle their infants at birth, to save them the fate of slavery. Of motherhood she writes with great sensitivity; in the poem "In My Name" she penetrates the ambivalence that pervades a woman who is about to bear a child conceived in rape and hate:

> Heavy with child
> belly
> an arc
> of black moon

I squat over
dry plantain leaves

and command the earth
to receive you

in my name
in my blood

to receive you
my curled bean

my tainted

perfect child

> my bastard fruit
> my seedling
> my sea grape
> my strange mulatto
> my little bloodling

Let the snake slipping in deep grass
be dumb before you

Let the centipede writhe and shrivel
in its tracks

Let the evil one strangle on his own tongue
even as he sets his eyes upon you

For with my blood
I've cleansed you
and with my tears
I've pooled the river Niger

now my sweet one it is for you to swim

Grace Nichols lives in her characters; she says things for them which they would not have been able to put into words for themselves in their crowded lives – in their capture from Africa, in the Middle Passage, in the burdened slavery days and in the deprived years after abolition. She gives them language to describe the feelings they endured. When she steps out of their lives she wonders in simple words at the immensity of their sacrifice. Her work eschews vehemence and anger in a way that leaves you aching and wondering. Her themes are commonplace and particular to the experiences of Blackwomen. Two other new and exciting poetry books are Merle Collins' *Because the Dawn Breaks* and Iyamidè Hazely's *Ripples and Jagged Edges*.

There are still too few published novelists among us. To date, the best known is Nigerian-born Buchi Emecheta, a prolific writer of adult and children's books. Some of these are autobiographical, based on her life mainly in Britain; these include the novels *In the Ditch* (1972) and *Second-Class Citizen* (1977), and her autobiograhy *Head Above Water* (1986). Other novels of hers such as *The Bride Price* (1976) and *The Slave Girl* (1979) draw on African experiences. All her writing is preoccupied with the condition of woman, whether in Africa or Britain. The autobiographical novels trace the problems of adjustment for an immigrant family – the weather, housing difficulties, white racism, family relationships, etc. Her most recent autobiographical book is *Head Above Water* (1986). It marks the turning point in her life, for in it she celebrates her triumphs and the whole book is permeated with a spirit of joy. In most of Emecheta's other books, what stands out most is her perception of the way in which African traditional culture determines women's lives, notably in *The Joys of Motherhood* (1982). Powerful as this novel is, one senses that she is not campaigning, as such, against the power of malevolent men. She does not directly attack male power though she observes how secure men are in their rights as compared to the precarious position of women. What she is doing for African women is breaking the taboo, the pretence that they are secure and contented. She denounces this fallacy loudly, and openly shows the social injustices against women and girls, while exposing the complicity of womanhood in the perpetuation of the system. Examining the role of women necessarily tackles what lies deeply buried in the primordial traditions of religion and social structure. Colonialism also added its own dimension. Men whose authority has been undermined have tended to hold on tight to the vestiges of power they can still wield. For African women this has created a hierarchical view of liberation; they have to ask themselves which liberation struggle should be taken on first. The majority of them have viewed the imbalances in the ordering of their societies as though they were objective, God-given injunctions, and they have endured it all as though it were inevitable, with resigned acceptance.

In *The Joys of Motherhood* Emecheta maps out a wide area of African society, covering the traditional setting as well as the turbulent life style of urban Africans. She deals with topics such as polygamy, childlessness, differing attitudes to boys and girls and, paradoxically, the pains of motherhood. In Africa children are the centre of existence. Failure to conceive robs a woman of status and casts doubt on her morals: "When a woman is virtuous, it is easy for her to conceive." Inability to do so condemns her to absolute failure and ultimate humiliation —and she can be treated with savage brutality. Several of Emecheta's women suffer untold mental torture for failing to fulfil that role of motherhood.

Not only is there pressure on a woman to become pregnant, and as soon after marriage as possible, there is also a demand on her to bear male offspring: "Our life starts from immortality and ends in immortality . . . I know you have children, but they are girls, who in a few years' time will go and help build another man's immortality." One might think that women, the instruments of such immortality, would in return be venerated; but this is not the case. That very power to link man with the unreachable – her sexuality – often condemns a woman to persecution. It is such illogical and harsh attitudes in African society that Emecheta spotlights. Why cannot a woman be valued in her own right? Can she only learn the gift of a successful marriage through bearing children? "God, when will you create a woman who will be fulfilled in herself, a full human being, not anyone's appendage?" wonders Emecheta's heroine Nnu Ego. And then, having given birth to children, her responsibilities towards them become a bind: "Her love and duty for her children were like her chain of slavery." All because she was the mother of three sons, "she was supposed to be happy in her poverty, in her nail-biting agony, in her churning stomach, in her rage, in her cramped room . . . oh, it was a confusing world." The notion of male superiority is equally damaging for boys, though in a different way. They inherit the received opinion that they are superior to girls – and to grown women, for that matter. They grow up entertaining the feeling that even if they fail in all areas of human responsibility they remain superior to women, and this gives them a false sense of complacency.

For most women of Africa, however, the deepest hurt remains polygamy; it is mainly on account of this practice that hearts are broken. African wives are not expected to feel jealous. If they do, they must not acknowledge it or let anyone know. Emecheta allows her protagonist, Nnu Ego, the full expression of jealousy when, overnight, her family swells as a new wife walks in with her children and takes over her bed and her husband. She has to lie awake and endure the noises of their lovemaking within earshot. All this is within the context of a turbulent change in Africa's social history – the city slum experience that has drastically reduced male authority. Husbands can no longer claim to be the sole supporters of their families. Women contribute as much as they can towards the family income, yet men seem unwilling to recognize this shift.

Buchi Emecheta knows the hidden feelings of African women and she voices them as perhaps no one has done before. Where the African woman has made a virtue of silent suffering, Emecheta exposes the conspiracy, insisting that female complacency and unquestioning acceptance of male domination do not constitute the quintessence of morality. It is women who impose order on other younger women through various tactics; ostracism, scapegoating and witch-hunting. And so women continue to empower men to abuse them. At the end of *The Joys of Motherhood* Emecheta makes no pretence about the African woman setting herself free. Nnu Ego dies alone, foiled and unloved and back where she started. It is as if she never went away, never made a move in terms of the conditions of women. Her daughters are regarded in much the same way as African women were in the past. No triumph, no possibilities, just the recognition of what it means to be an African woman.

Joan Riley has two novels to her credit – *The Unbelonging* (1985) and *Waiting in the Twilight* (1987). *The Unbelonging* merits a closer look for its approach lends itself to an interesting interpretation. A story about childhood, family separations, incestuous relationships and racism, it is a study in guilt and fear and violence. At times it reads like autobiography though Joan Riley assures us that it is not; she has worked among Black youngsters in children's homes and says that the inspiration for her book derived from observations of these. The novel is permeated with a sense of powerlessness on the part of the young protagonist, Hyacinth Williams, who displays strong negative feelings towards Black people in general and herself in particular – an ambivalence that is best understood in psychological terms. The book is marked by a total absence of protest. It vividly depicts the victimization of a young Black girl and exposes the ravages of sexist violence in the community.

Hyacinth arrives in Britain at the age of eleven, at which point her life seems to grind to a halt. She comes to join her father, his woman and her children in a cold, loveless home. But worst of all, she is subjected to her father's incestuous attentions. From then on she lives in various children's institutions and suffers extreme loneliness and racial hostility from children and adults alike. Her father is himself an immigrant and a victim of poverty and racism. There is no apparent support for the family from the community in the form of friends and neighbours or an active social life. His whole existence lies between home, work and home again. Although he drinks, there is no evidence of visits to the pub; he drinks at home. On his visit to the doctor with Hyacinth, we witness a cowed character, almost servile, who betrays ingrained feelings of inferiority. Because he is himself a victim, he in his turn abuses whom he can: his "wife" and his daughter. So when she first arrives, Hyacinth is entrapped in the pitiless home. She has to cope with her father's aggressive antagonism as well as with a very hostile environment – the weather, the slum and the school.

If *The Unbelonging* is not about physical rape, it is certainly about a social and psychological rape. From the first page, Hyacinth lives with the dream that she was once loved and is still loved by her aunt, that in that aunt she has a family and home. The reader goes through the novel believing this and wishing with Hyacinth that she will find her way back "home" – only to discover in the end, when she does return to the Caribbean, that there is no home for her. One has the impression that there never was any reality, that it was all a dream – perhaps a necessary dream of escape.

But the novel itself can be taken as being symbolic of the Black experience in Britain. Perhaps this is its true value: tracing the desperately lonely existence of our people on their arrival in a community that will not accept them. It could be said that Hyacinth's abortive return "home" parallels the way we no longer belong even to our so-called homes in the Caribbean and Africa, after the long years away. If this is the case, the novel is saying a great deal about our own unbelonging. Many members of our community in Britain today came here as children, those who followed after their parents, like Joan Riley and Hyacinth. These people may well feel they do not entirely belong; they have another home, their home of origin, no matter how young they were when they left it. Yet the great majority of Black youth are British-born and yet they too feel they do not belong, at least not emotionally. They feel sufficiently estranged not to regard Britain as a permanent home, even though they have no other experience to which to relate. This is due to the attitudes of the host society towards all Black people, old and young, British or not. *The Unbelonging* is about this schizophrenic existence. If our writings are rooted in our experiences and are a reflection of our life, then this is indeed a novel that deserves to be taken seriously. Riley's book does not climax and has no neat ending. We leave Hyacinth in the streets of Jamaica, wondering where to go next, for her problem is not resolved. It is maybe inevitable that a novel like this should come out of the Black experience in Britain – an innovative, cyclical novel where people are caught up in a whirl of events without resolution.

Before 1986, a sprinkling of poems by a few Blackwomen featured lesbianism without focusing too strongly on the theme. But with the publication in mid-1986 of Barbara Burford's collection of short stories *The Threshing Floor* the subject has erupted on the scene with such force that the category of Black writing from a lesbian perspective in Britain has become of great significance.

Burford's book is remarkable, first and foremost, for its beauty and its sensitivity. It takes its proud place as a Black woman's book both for its note of independence and, in its title story, for its perception of lesbianism. Unusually, "The Threshing Floor" (which constitutes half the book) is set in the heart of British society, mainly in the University of Canterbury and in that city, away from the big urban ghettos. Perhaps in this sense it could be said to be more British than others of our writings, for it confronts white society with the Black presence as an accomplished fact. In this way, more than any other, it is futuristic. Black and white women mix freely, so that the reader almost loses interest in the colour of the various characters. Similarly, university professionals rub shoulders with non-academics without letting this distinction intrude on their relationship as men and women and artists and business people.

Burford's novella is a simple story of love and loss and love again. The loss of a great love through death affords the writer the opportunity to reveal the strength and depth of lesbian relationships. What is striking about this treatment of the subject is that it is not viewed against the backdrop of the wider society. We are not comparing or contrasting the world of lesbians with that of heterosexuals. Lesbianism as treated here assumes its own authenticity and does not seek justification or acceptance. Instead it stands as an immutable fact of life. This is the feeling that the reader gets. The writer's approach even muzzles the kind of curiosity that may attend close scrutiny of homosexuality. Many works on this subject have tended to affirm the prevailing view of lesbianism as an asocial development, and lesbian writers have struggled to legitimize their life in this society and have sought acceptance in the face of rejection.

Whereas the other stories of her collection deal with life in Britain as it affects Blackwomen "The Threshing Floor" makes little reference to the wider community. Burford takes it as read that within society there are married couples, heterosexual men and women, some single and some cohabiting, as well as lesbians and homosexual men, some of whom might like to marry were it permissible. In this story she chooses to deal with the issue of lesbianism separately as a manifestation of human variety, richness and expression. She does not specifically renounce heterosexual family life but she strips it of its paramountcy, its prerogative as the sole basis for inter-personal relations; she simply ignores and therefore undermines it. Nowhere in the book is there a nuclear family based on the 'norm' of husband, wife and children. One or two such families are shadowy in the background, for example Elaine and Roy and their child. In fact we scarcely meet Roy and the child. It is Elaine who materializes as a friend of Hannah's in her time of need. There is also Grace and Douglas, who hang like pictures on a wall, to convince us that Hannah's dead lover Jenny did have a family. Somewhere on the edge of things these couples stand, unable to defend the family institution as viable and authentic. Hannah herself, the chief protagonist, does not know family life, having been brought up in care in a children's home. The condition of the unwanted child that she is implies in itself the failure of the traditional family.

None of the women in the Cantii Glass co-operative make any significant reference to being married or having male friends. By contrast, at least two important characters reveal failed relationships with men: Caro with her child Zhora, and Marah who falls in love with Hannah at the end of the story, after the break-down of her marriage to Keith. Men are not attacked or denounced directly. The only allusion that could be construed as such is when Caro asserts: ". . . in many ways she'd be safer with you . . . men can be such shits . . ." Caro and Judith (Jenny's mother) are the only women to show some reservation about lesbianism. But when Caro relents, conceding that Marah would be happier with Hannah than with any man who might give her the child she so desperately wants, she validates the lesbian choice. Although only one lesbian relationship figures large, the impression is of being in a lesbian society. Everyone seems to affirm it. Burford is at pains to show that without men, women's relationships are generous, helpful, considerate, reliable, dependable, sharing, and that satisfaction in love and work and business and between social classes is humanly possible.

By inference she shows that it is men who bring out the worst in women, making them competitive and jealous.

Having said all this, there is something ironic about the absence of a live lesbian relationship in the book. We know of the intensity of the love between Jenny and Hannah; but we live in retrospect, in its burning memory. It died with Jenny. We see it through the cold moonlight that floods through her room dimly through the veil of tears in Hannah's eyes. Hannah, left behind, seems to avoid involvement in other possible relationships, ostensibly to show how great the dead relationship was. Right at the end of the book we see her make a new commitment to Marah. But the reader feels cheated of yet another love which might prosper and become vibrant in the future, as it were behind the reader's back. To some extent, this avoidance is paralleled by Burford's treatment of colour issues in "The Threshing Floor". Colour as a quality has beautiful associations – not surprising in a story about artists. It enhances the crafted glass that the women make; it is a beautiful presence in Marah's tapestries and in the incisions of the sun and moon that we see both in Jenny's room and Marah's work-room. Colour is both positive and affirmative. Yet as a social and political factor in this story (by contrast with others in the book) colour is in neutral tones. There are stabbing references to the inconvenience that it can cause, such as "Jenny Harrison and her darkie woman . . ." Hannah is disturbed that Jenny had to love her across the colour barrier: "A woman who had been insistently brave enough to ask that they not only accept her reality, but the reality of the black woman whom she loved." Although Burford makes the effort to build a small community of Black characters around Hannah – Cora and Zhora and Marah – so that they form a social unit, they apparently confront none of the racial problems that attend most Black people in this society. In this novella Burford blurs the borders of sex and colour, redrawing the social map to create her characters' world.

Other novels that have been published recently include Merle Collins' *Angel*, based on a period of political and social change in Granada over the last thirty years and the involvement of three generations of women in that change. Zoë Wicomb's novel *You Can't Get Lost in Cape Town* is about a young woman's return to South Africa in order to come to terms with her rejected racial inheritance.

The varied textures of our lives are powerfully revealed by the writing collective of Stella Dadzie, Beverley Bryan and Suzanne Scafe in their bestselling book *The Heart of the Race: Black Women's Lives in Britain* (1985). This is a fine, well researched work, a landmark in our progress. It charts the historical contours of our lives in this country – immigration, followed by the disappointments, the isolation, the rejection and the struggle to hold on even when things were hard. It portrays our galvanized approach to a harsh reception, shows how in many ways we were pivotal in our communities and are the mainstay in the bitter struggle against oppression. The book describes our contribution to labour, as workers and trade unionists; our role in the National Health Service; our opposition to the racist education system; and how we fare in the welfare state. But, above all, it reveals our responses to all these – how we have organized and opposed all forms of intimidatory practices and legislation. It focuses, as has never been done before, on the political strength of Blackwomen and their refusal to be browbeaten by a callous system. We have been the spearhead in organizing against racist attacks by the police in their use of such measures as the "Sus" law against our youth. We have formed defence committees for those who are victimized by the law, and we have joined housing campaigns and supported innumerable community issues. A book that so clearly spells out the contributions of Blackwomen forces society to acknowledge our vital role and fosters a sense of worth in us.

Another valuable work of non-fiction is *Black Women: Bringing It All Back Home* (1980), by Margaret Prescod-Roberts and Norma Steel. Exploring the implications of emigration and immigration, the book highlights women's role in protecting entire families from the rigours of adapting to new surroundings and keeping ties with those left behind. Above all, the authors argue the legitimacy of Black families moving in large numbers to settle in Britain or North America. We had every right to move, for although we had worked hard in our former communities, generating wealth in the Caribbean over hundreds of years, we had been left poor. All the wealth we made was stripped away and taken to these "mother" countries. We came to share the wealth that we ourselves had created, claiming what was legitimately ours.

Our writing is all the time widening in scope, witnessed by new works such as: *Black Women Talk*, an anthology of poetry edited by a group of women – Da Choong, Olivette Cole Wilson, Bernadine Evaristo and Gabriella Pearse; *A Dangerous Knowing*, the poetry of Barbara Burford, Jackie Kay, Grace Nichols and Gabriella Pearse; *Charting the Journey: Writings by Black and Third World Women*; and Jackie Kay's play, *Chiarascuro*, which has been performed but not yet published. Also recently published is *Brickbats and Bouquets: Black Woman's Critique*, a compilation of book, theatre and film reviews written by *Race Today*'s Arts Editor Akua Rugg. So far, however, there has been little material produced especially for Black children. Among the first writers in this genre is Petronella Breinbrug with her popular "Sean" series – *My Brother Sean*, *Doctor Sean* and *Sean's Red Bike*, followed by *Sally-Anne's Umbrella*. Other books for and about children include Buchi Emecheta's *Tich*, *The Cat*, *Nowhere to Play* and *The Wrestling Match*, and more recently Grace Nichols' *Trust You*, *Wriggly* and *Baby Fish and Other Stories*. But what is more significant is that young people are themselves showing increasing interest in writing. ACER (Afro-Caribbean Educational Resources), a project funded by the Inner London Education Authority, has done much to encourage young talent; each year the best pieces submitted for their Black Young Writers Awards are compiled into an anthology. A young poet with two volumes to her credit at a very early age is Accabre Huntley. Her first collection, *At School Today*, was published when she was ten years old and her second, *Easter Monday Blues*, when she was sixteen. Her earlier poems were mainly about her childhood world of family, friends and school. They already showed an awareness of the lot of Black people in British society, but also a healthy determination to live a normal happy childhood:

> I am black as I thought
> My lids are brown as
> I thought
> My hair is curled as I
> thought
> I am free as I know.

The written word, according to traditional Western values, informs society, for it is pregnant with knowledge and truth. It is the primary means of communicating ideas, creating the possibility of change as it confronts the status quo and poses challenges. This power of the written word naturally reflects on the writer, for it is the writer who generates the body of thought that not only forces people to take note of what is said but of who says it. Perhaps for this reason, few people were prepared to accord the authority and the written word to Blackwomen. On the British literary scene we have for a long time been in the shadows – not because we have not been writing and expressing ourselves but rather because white Britain has done its best to cold-shoulder us. For some people the association of Blackwomen with the art of writing still strains credulity, and they have found it difficult to give us recognition as writers, for in their minds we remain fettered to the images of the past that saw us as calloused, mindless drudges.

The book industry as a whole – publishers, distributors and retailers – is highly regulated because it constitutes the body of knowledge and values generally called British civilization. Publishers are the guard dogs of their great tradition. They have the unquestionable power to determine which writers appear in print, what subjects are treated by whom at any given time. They determine the "standards" in the profession. The implication that some books are more valid than others (some values more valid than others) augurs badly for Black writing in general and for Blackwomen's writing in particular. The British establishment jealously stands ready to supppress anything that deviates from "the truth" or reflects unfavourably on conservative beliefs which were formed and preserved in the dim past, without consideration for our reality. It follows therefore that the values encoded in the literature and enshrined in the laws of Britain often have little validity for Black society. Throughout the history of slavery and colonialism, Black knowledge and values were brutally stigmatized, and although we hold on to the shreds of that former heritage we witness a strong reluctance on the part of white society to reinstate or accommodate it. The subjective intervention on the part of publishers may affect our expression as writers in our effort to conform, confining our ideas to those acceptable to white society. By so doing, we abdicate our duty to our own communities. Besides achieving the death of our culture, this kills off our individual originality and creativity. Writing under such cultural domination, the Blackwoman is pressured by three conflicting motives: the instinct to write for its own sake, the artist for herself; the demand to keep faith with our own society; and the need to defend our culture against further erosion.

Notwithstanding the general attitudes of mainstream commercial publishers, the picture would be incomplete if no mention were made of certain exceptional developments taking place within the publishing world. Much of it has little to do specifically with Blackwomen writers, but its effects, like ripples in a pool, touch us indirectly. During the past decade and a half there have been changes in the outlook of white, male-dominated publishers which would have rocked the industry were it not so well secured through power, finance and tradition. First the feminist lobby has pressured them into promoting women who, in the main, worked on sufferance within these companies. This, being a case of too little too late for some enterprising women, led to the founding of feminist publishing houses. Initially these too seemed to have no thought for the beleaguered Blackwoman writer, their paramount consideration being to serve the neglected needs of their marginalized fellow white sisters. It has taken the literary cloudburst of Blackwomen's writing from North America to force Britain's feminist presses to look nearer home for Black talent.

Until recently, few publishing houses concerned themselves with Third World writing: the handful who did include Longman, Heinemann and Macmillan, and even they produced almost entirely for the export market. The doors have widened somewhat to admit Blackwomen to the lists of prestigious houses such as Virago, The Women's Press, Zed Press and others. In addition, there is a growing number of small Black companies producing books by our women. One of the oldest is Bogle-L'Ouverture Publications, begun by Jessica Huntley. Another woman who has started her own company, publishing her own work, is Buchi Emecheta. And in 1987 we have seen yet another women's publishing house, Zora Press established by Iyamidè Hazeley and Adeola Solanke. Joining the swelling ranks of committed Black publishers, headed by the now long-established New Beacon Books, are Karnak House, Akira and Karia. We owe a debt to these fledgling Black concerns, as well as to the radical white presses who first provided an outlet for some of our now better known writers.

The books that Blackwomen do write are invariably considered a separate class of writing that is somehow discredited, less authentic, not part of the main body of literature. More often than not, they will be stocked mainly by alternative booksellers. This discrimination means that our books do not easily find their way into schools and universities, for their validity is in doubt. Organizations such as the Association for the Teaching of Caribbean and African and Asian Literature (ATCAL) have been formed by teachers and others with a particular interest in trying to change these prevailing attitudes. Having been in existence for several years, ATCAL has made slow progress in achieving its main aim – to convince the examining bodies to accord examination status to this literature, for it is essential for the young of whatever race to understand the Black experience.

There was a time when Blackwomen did feature in British literature, portrayed as cardboard characters with no life of our own. Interestingly, we were never shown working in the fields in the period of slavery or as beasts of burden in the colonial era; somehow this reality failed to rear its ugly head in that fine literature. The debased roles in which we were depicted took no cognizance of our fullness and our potential. In short, our reality was denied even then. Rather, a more tempered image was painted. We appeared as harmlessly useful females, jolly house servants in nurturing roles, sex objects for lustful white males in those puritanical days. This image lingers on in many minds. On the whole, however, it is as if white Britons want to forget the past, to forget that once we lived in close proximity with them, in their kitchens, caring for their children, being raped by their men and then bearing those tainted babies – most of this, of course, away from British soil. It is hardly surprising that our appearance in the front garden of Britain causes embarrassment. We bring back to life forgotten crimes and immense guilt, and British society would as soon wipe us out along with the shameful memory. Search the wider literary scene as one may, one is hard put to find anything relating to Blackwomen today. We are acutely aware of this, of the fact that having served our former purpose, we have for historical, social and psychological reasons slipped into the subsconscious of our erstwhile masters. This amnesia is the unacknowledged admission that British society has still not come to terms with our presence. We linger in a kind of social limbo and consequently suffer a state of invisibility.

It behoves us to define our position not as others see us but as we ourselves identify our reality. Clear self-definition should release the potential in us that alone will help us survive the onslaught of hostile forces ranged against us. We seek to keep the continuity of the Black experience from Africa to the Caribbean, from the Caribbean to the streets of Britain, linking generations in search of our identity, seeking to demonstrate an independent view of our reality. Herein lies the only possibility of healing the scars of our history and our present.

Black people are now irrevocably part of Britain; our presence on these shores goes back centuries. We came originally to serve, creating the wealth of Britian, first as slaves and later as workers. Stories of the reception of those early settlers are chilling. Today we are a well-established community. We have always been in the minority, but it is not our minority status that gives rise to many of our problems. In measuring Black/white relations, it has been established that the majority/minority scale is not a prime consideration; present-day South

Africa serves as glaring proof of that, and other minority groups in Britain enjoy an undifferentiated status. It is in the minds of the white British that the problem lies. In their perception of us we have been captured and pegged to a history that will not change.

As a largely migrant community we are well-travelled, with a wide spectrum of experience of other life-styles. The very decision we had to take to migrate in search of better opportunities proves that ours is a community with a potential and a capacity to fight against odds and to overcome. Those early immigrants were not a random sample from their societies. Only a select few could rise in response to such challenges.

The majority of our community are people of Caribbean extraction, whose history is littered with tokens of victory throughout the years of bondage. Whether Western historians sweep this history under the carpet or not, it continues to fire our confidence in our ability to change things for the better. We know that the abolition of slavery was not an altogether philanthropic exercise; it came about when the mass of those enslaved were no longer prepared to make the system work profitably. The ongoing sabotage among slaves, the subversions, the memorable Caribbean rebellion under the leadership of Toussaint L'Ouverture, all led to the breakdown of that nefarious system of exploitation. Our history of resistance enables us to face the future. The fibre of our people is borne out by the momentous resolution, on a mass scale, to brave the unknown and come to Britain in large numbers back in the 1950s and 1960s. Those who came then pursued a dream. History is made by dreamers. It is on this pioneering spirit that Britain is now trampling.

The other substantial part of our community consists of those who came from Africa at a time when colonialism was finally loosening its grip on that continent. Most came as students to acquire skills necessary to run their own newly liberated countries in the late 1950s and 1960s. These Africans had already overcome great odds in their own countries. They had needed not only the money that the acquisition of education there presupposed but also to prove themselves intellectually able to join the élite who deserved further training overseas. Education had been in the hands of missionaries, select middle-class members of Western society who, being well disposed towards their pupils and anxious to fulfil their mission of "civilizing" the subject people, had created a thirst for learning among those they taught. At the same time they had given a taste for middle-class values. These newly inculcated values gave rise to a new outlook, an outward-bound expectation of life, within the grasp of young African men and women.

This then is a summary of the constituent members of the Black community in Britain today – a community drawn by various forces, if not chance, from different parts of the world. Most of them are not victims of war, nor were they driven to escape the fury of dictators in their native countries. They did not come because they had failed to adapt elsewhere; they came precisely because they were capable of adapting anywhere. They came because they were strong, if poor. They came, after World War II, to help a country in need of their services and so to meet their own needs. By and large, they share a common quality in their nature and outlook.

At first the Africans who had come to study and to be galvanized for their roles in their newly decolonized countries were given every facility to polish their skills, their attitudes, to learn to think British, before being shipped home to make their compatriots think British too. But those who ran out of money halfway through their courses or failed to measure up to the requirements of their studies tended to remain, in the hope that their fortunes would change. They did not alter their outlook, nor their aspirations. They were frustrated, but they went on expecting great things of themselves. They were still an upward-looking group.

However, the great potential of the Caribbeans and the Africans did not shine through. Our ambitions went unrecognized, for our outward trappings betrayed all our hopes. As we soon discovered, we had walked into a system that judged people by their speech, their dress, their occupation and their neighbourhood. We were judged not only by our financial standing but also by our history and by our colour. To the host community we were ex-savages and the descendants of slaves. We walked into a situation where our "notoriety" had gone before us in the much-heralded writings of adventurers and colonists, painting us in the "half-human and half-child" image. So we were readily shuffled into our "proper" social position to find our own level, a peculiar level set below all others – the working-Black-class. Things were put in motion to groom us for the British scene, to assimilate us, above all to make us accustomed to our new class. But we did not accept this. We set our sights on forbidden pastures, aspiring for our children or grandchildren to be electricians and town planners, lawyers, accountants or doctors.

We focused on our ambitions, refusing to be dampened, even when the sterile reality confronted us. This optimism was inevitable: having reached the lowest rung of social degradation as the dispossesed under slavery and colonialism, we could fall no further. The Black reality compels us to look up, not to accept to stay at the bottom. We go on transmitting high hopes to our children, but the crux of the problem is that the aspirations of this working-Black-class go unheeded by the host society, dismissed as proof enough that we lack a sense of reality (their reality). What we still lack, however, is the voice to communicate our reality and insist that it be heard. Our desires and expectations, strong as they are, are spoken only around our hearths in the ghettos. This is the heart of the conflict between the immigrant community and the host society. We are expected to be docile and satisfied with our lot; they cannot understand our discontent with our accorded place in society. If the white working class accepts its position – why don't we? This seems to be the question in the minds of many in authority. Teachers and careers officers do not take our children seriously when they disclose their career preferences; firmly the children are told not to aim so high. To make certain that their dreams are shattered once and for all, the education gate-keeping policy becomes more vigilant – few pass through. When it comes to employment the situation has been compounded by the effective controls in education. Black school-leavers seeking work are, in the majority, inadequately qualified. Poor education attainment guarantees that our young are unlikely to become a threat in the job market, are never going to be an economic/class threat.

Racial oppression is often measured in terms of the abuse we suffer or even the assaults made on us by the police. These are indeed serious aspects, sometimes culminating in death or maiming, as in the cases of Mrs Cynthia Jarrett or Mrs Cherry Groce. But a second look reveals the true forces governing our oppression. Those who manipulate the controls are in the financial institutions, the education system and the legal/judicial sector. Their power to subordinate us operates just below the surface of the legislature and the executive departments. Without parliament openly legislating against Black people as they do in South Africa, the ethos of the whole society is yet charged with hostility, if not open injustice. And indeed the Commonwealth Immigration Acts (1962–1983) have many clauses clearly drafted against Afro-Caribbean and Asian people.

While parliament may be seen to have clean hands in terms of direct machinations, the underhanded operation of discrimination is left to institutions and bodies and individuals. It is the fault of a particular bank or private concern, not banking law; it is the solicitor, not judicial law; it is the teacher, not the education authority. Yet one senses distinctly that this is not a matter of random prejudice; it seems officially sanctioned. Built into the very fibre of our society is a pervading sense of separateness, and Blacks are still targets for racial violence at the hands of the British public and police.

Most progressive peoples of the world work for a society with an equitable distribution of property and wealth. Given a choice, we should strive for a just society, rather than simply for a stake in the capitalist system. But the choice of changing the machinery and outlook of the state remains the preserve of the powerful majority and not a matter to be decided by a minority such as we are. British society as a whole has never shown a lasting inclination away from capitalism towards socialism and so long as the Black minority is entrapped in a capitalist society, so long as they participate in it, they will be oppressed by it. It is Hobson's choice: to operate within the structures of an oppressive capitalism, or to opt out.

Ownership of property in this society determines social position. Our inability to operate freely to acquire property echoes the past. The desire to own property is understandable: over and above any economic advantages, owning property affirms a sense of freedom. While we were enslaved, our position determined that we could own nothing. The badge of slavery is not only the inability to own property, but being property yourself. Though we were freed from slavery, at least in the statute books, Britain's failure to open its doors to free enterprise to Black people is a serious attempt to nullify our real freedom. Slavery has to do with two sets of people, the slavers and the enslaved. It also operates on two levels – the physical and the psychological. It is impossible to ignore the scars left in the minds of both the ex-slave and the ex-slaver. Long after slavery was abolished by law, we see these former adversaries wrestling with their antagonisms. The return from slavery is as arduous a journey as the road into slavery. Organizations such as the Ku-Klux-Klan in America clearly show how hard it is to let go, once a slaver. Long after the slave is free, the ex-slaver will be engaged in staying the progress of that freedom, to keep the ex-slave in his or her expected place – at the ex-master's feet, if not under them.

Our experience in Britain reveals that, a hundred years after abolition, many people hold on relentlessly to the ideals of slavery. Not just as workers do they exclude us as full participants; more importantly, they begrudge us access to vital commercial and industrial structures. We are caught in the vice of the twin instruments upholding this society: the banking system and the legal system. Somewhere in the operations of these two is the conspiracy, the collective intrigue, to curtail our right to participate in business. The banker's built-in attitude tells him his money is not safe in the hands of Blacks. His decision is based not on having been let down by them in the past, nor on his assessment of the Black individual who approaches him, but is arrived at using a stereotypic measure. There is no reasonable cause for his doubts. Seldom do Blacks appear in the courts or the media linked with cases of a financial nature, fraud, embezzlements of funds, for they seldom come anywhere near the management of large sums of money. Yet the legacy of the past is that the managers of financial institutions still find it difficult to consider as a possible equation Blacks = business = success. So they are loath to let us try and we are fated only to work for others when they will let us. The few of us who are in any form of business invariably get there by pooling the paltry resources of family or friends. And, since they cannot rely on bank loan facilities when cashflow problems arise, it is not hard to imagine the failure rate of such ventures.

The situation has its own side effect. It means that our money does not flow into the coffers of Black businesses; it cannot circulate to the specific benefit of the Black community. It cannot help generate more jobs among us. Rather than benefiting us, our spending power promotes the rest of society. Given the opportunity, we might just defy our chains and succeed, but then our economic self-reliance would pose a challenge to Britain's carefully worked out class system. We would become a threat not just to the white working class but to the middle class as well. We should get beyond control – who knows, even become powerful and "swamp" the country's structures of power. That would be unthinkable. So the Black applicant with any business proposition is dismissed out of hand.

The arguments I raise here may seem directed at individuals rather than institutions. This is in response to the peculiar brand of British oppression. In diplomacy, the British are past masters. They are able to maintain an unassailable parliamentary/legal system, yet be just as oppressive as some of the more blatant systems. In this way the oppressive system itself is individualized. Not a banker, not a housing officer, not a teacher can be absolved from their acts of prejudice for they cannot be said to be carrying out government policy. They are themselves willing instruments of the silent power of oppression. And because of this structure of oppression, members of the Black community suffer it more at an individual level than at a state level as, for example, they would in South Africa.

Alongside the intense struggle to reorientate socially and economically is the greater struggle to repossess our soul, devastated as we were by slavery and colonialism. Those experiences disrupted and mutilated our cultures and values. We lived under prohibitions then, without our languages and religions, without communal intercourse at any level. The ingenuity of our ancestors to regenerate, to contrive new ways of living, new languages, to adopt new religions and adapt to new communities, poses challenges today for us, the children of the oppressed. Our host society can have no way of knowing what it is to be on such a cultural march to recover our lost roots.

Considering how arduous this journey is, it might well have been easier to give up and adapt completely to the cultural structures of this society, had they but welcomed us in. They have not. The British have never been renowned for receiving people as guests and living peaceably with them. (Nor have they hardly ever regarded themselves as guests when they have gone to other countries. Yet every corner of the world today has the British as guests, and often much more than guests. Our forebears in various parts of the world lived with the British not as guests but as expropriating invaders.) Without resorting to outlandish schemes of exclusion such as South Africa's apartheid, they have effectively kept us out of their institutions – their churches, their institutes of higher learning, their business world, their parliament, their judiciary. The Black community has no option but to recover what it can of its identity. The host society has not always been sensitive to the urgent need for cultural identity as a vital component, a prerequisite for success in the education of each child. For years they did not realize that the policies of assimilation were undermining the value of the child and reducing that child's capacity to learn. There are those who are still dithering about policy relating to mother-tongue teaching, unable to accept our languages from Africa and the Caribbean. The various dialects of the Caribbean are not maimed English, but a creative reconstruction of language by people deprived of their own and thrown together in mute work teams. This is our language, and it should be accorded literary recognition.

The period after World War II when we came to Britain in large numbers was one of reconstruction, when women needed to work for both national and family reasons. For us this was nothing new; we have been in a period of reconstruction since slavery, reconstructing our lives with little help from the world community. Reconstruction has become a way of life. Our women must work if we are to survive. Our economic, social and political position makes it imperative. Given an alternative, we might not now want it otherwise, for through working we can assert our independence and claim a stake in society. But we have had to fight the racism and sexism of employers and trade unions alike. We have fought for self-respect against colleagues who display the undisguised racism of the British working class. We encounter hostility as Black workers and as working women, occupying the most menial jobs with correspondingly low wages and loss of dignity. We have turned to unions for help in fighting exploitation, poor wages and bad conditions. But those unions are as riddled with racism and sexism as other institutions.

Racism and sexism have frequently marked our labour relations over and above the issues of wages and conditions. Sometimes Afro-Caribbean women, aligned closely with Asian women, have taken on the whole weight of industrial labour relations against a reluctant legal system. Our men in their own way have also suffered badly, and our strong stand has encouraged them to join hands with us to fight a common enemy. This has demonstrated the possibility of eliminating sexism in dealing with matters of common concern; the Black Trade Unionist Solidarity Movement now has a declared policy that men and women work together as equals, with equal representation. Thus, racism has become a powerful prod in the fight for fair and just labour conditions.

It is not only outside the family that Blackwomen shoulder heavy responsibility and face hardship. The family, which suffered a merciless onslaught during slavery, over a hundred years later has not fully recovered. The institution of marriage suffered irreparable damage and motherhood itself was defiled. Were it not for the potential of motherhood, women's capacity to have children, we would most likely not have been taken into slavery with our men. We were enslaved because of this very sacred potential – not to raise our children with love and care in the service of our nations, but to breed more slaves. Whereas the African concept of motherhood valued attributes of strength, courage, self-reliance and endurance, under slavery we became more vulnerable precisely because of these qualities. The religious significance of continuity and creativity was brutalized in the deepest sense. In transit from Africa to the Americas and to the Caribbean, motherhood underwent a crippling transformation. In Britain today we encounter a further transformation. At every turn, it seems, motherhood is used to denigrate us. Where once we could not keep up with the slavers' demand for ever more children, we are now accused of "careless breeding", of lowering moral standards by disregarding marriage and popularizing single parenthood (this is said irrespective of changing views of morality throughout the Western world); we are blamed for bringing decline to British morals, and this has led to drastic measures to control our birth rate.

In considering the relations between the sexes in the Black community, it would be self-delusion to pretend that our problems are entirely due to slavery and racism. The patterns of relationships in any society are strongly embedded in that society's customs and traditions. Our roots in Britain reach back to life styles in Africa. The practices themselves may have been forgotten but the attitudes they engendered survive. Despite many of Africa's societies being matriarchal, which might imply a certain power for women, men remain very dominant. Women service societies, managing agriculture, producing and storing food and making substantial economic contributions. But this does not give them social, political or economic independence. The African woman works hard and whatever accrues to her goes to enhance her husband's status; it is not hers to strengthen her social position. The best it may do is command more respect from the husband, which in a polygamous situation is of course of great importance to a woman, for the more productive wife retains greater attention in this competitive situation. It will be appreciated, therefore, why polygamy is popular with men; it sets them as managers of productive teams of women who work hard to outdo each other for a man's favours. The long and short of this is that whether a society is matriarchal or patriarchal, the position of women is broadly similar throughout Africa. It is these attitudes that were transported to the Carribean and other places so long ago.

And looking at Black male/female relationships in Britain today one sees rudiments of behaviour which is African in origin. This is not to minimize the way in which slavery whittled away the traditional power of our men, giving nothing in exchange. The British experience has not improved the situation, since our self-regard is under constant racist attack, especially at work. The resulting build-up of frustration and aggression has no social outlet. Black unemployment is high compared with the rest of the population and this has many implications. It makes it hard for Blackmen to fulfil their responsibility within the family. Those who know unemployment will realize what this means for the whole ethos of family life, affecting not just the financial aspect but also the emotional, inducing hostility or even aggression. Families break down under the stress. The disruption of Black family life is due largely to our loss of dignity at the hands of white society.

The majority of our youth leave school with few prospects of a job that might enable them to settle down, marry and start a self-respecting family life. These unemployed young people, with abundant vitality and frustration, often start early families. Whether intended or not, this can solve some problems for these captive couples: the young mother and her baby may be given a home and maintenance by the social services. The popular image of "irresponsible" young men and unmarried mothers disregards the devastation on these young lives. The picture of them as scroungers on the social security system is of society's own making. From the moment the state forces the father into a situation where he cannot in all honour take full responsibility as a family man, he is reduced to being a "cowboy" father who only calls to see the child and the mother at *her* new home when he can. His social and psychological condition is lowered. She provides a home for the baby, while he keeps away because he is unable to find a job and thus cannot provide much. It is not surprising that such relationships break up. This situation leaves women saddled with greater responsibility for the home and parenthood, not just at this stage but throughout their lives. Mothers have become pivotal, not by choice but through the mechanics of social engineering.

In the Black community it is essential that most of our women should work. This gives rise to problems of child-minding and fostering. Child-minding, which in any circumstances is not ideal, is fraught with problems. There is always the danger of a racist child-minder who would show little love for the child while accepting the task for the money. The standard of care can be low and can cause a great deal of damage to the child, both physically and psychologically. Buchi Emecheta explores this area in her book *Second-Class Citizen*. But even where the home and the minders are good and loving, there are other ramifications for the child's long-term development. Such children often exhibit problems of self-identity which eventually have a bearing on psychological and educational potential. They may suffer estrangement from their parents and identify more with the white family. Where fostering is concerned, the whole experience can be extremely traumatic for the child.

Having asserted that the Blackwoman is dominant in family life in the British context, one hastens to add that this is relative to her white counterpart, on the one hand, and to the traditionally passive African woman on the other. It does not imply that we have won the sex war, simply that we are resolved to do anything and everything to support ourselves. Similarly, it would be wrong to assume that young unwed parenthood typifies Black family life.

Although a primary cause of the disruption of Black family life is the Blackman's loss of dignity at the hands of white society and the capitalist system, one should not be tempted to use this as the sole reason for incompetence in our men, or gloss over the difficulties in Black male/female relationships. Of course the sex war goes on quite apart from the complicity of white society. In the writings of Blackwomen in Britain the treatment of men is surprisingly lenient and less disparaging than one might expect – certainly they are not targeted for criticism. There seems a deliberate effort not to belittle them. This conscious self-censoring is protective of the whole society: the desire not to "let the side down" – a sharing of the pain of racism, which is ultimately the major cause of domestic troubles. In our writings we look searchingly at our community, seeking strengths rather than weaknesses, bringing out less of the antagonism and more of the togetherness between men and women. Few of us are openly critical of our men. A notable exception is to be found in the work of Iyamidè Hazeley, a fine example of an accomplished writer-performer. She has recently published her new book *Ripples and Jagged Edges* and to do it she co-founded a publishing house of her own with Ade Solanke called Zora Press. In her poem "Political Unity", she says:

You call me "Sister", Brother,
yet it seems you speak with the empty kernel of the word,
And sometimes
When you talk to me
there lingers after
a void
far more empty than existed before.
When you hear my anguished silence and are reassured by it
    then I know that our strength depends on my becoming weak
    that you have not questioned
the bars, deeply entrenched,
of the barbed cage, externally defined,
that is the oppressor's role you so emulate.

The sometimes conciliatory tone in our writings about men contrasts sharply with the views one picks up in conversation with Blackwomen of all ages which are far more virulent and open. It is also true that few of us are feminists in the sense understood by white middle-class women. Ours is an ambivalent position where we may be strongly critical of our men's assertive sexism and their failure to assume their share of responsibility in our communities burdened with racism; yet we are protective of them, not wanting them attacked by other women (particularly white women) or even grouped with other men for their sexism. At the root of this ambivalence is the question of inequality between the races. The oppressive white man and the oppressed Blackman may both exhibit sexist behaviour, but the former does so from a position of power, the latter from a position of powerlessness. This creates a disparity in the quality of that sexism and even in the minds of women on the receiving end of it. A white man does not oppress a Blackwoman in exactly the same way as he does a white woman. Similarly, a Blackman behaves differently when dealing with a white woman rather than a Blackwoman; with the white woman he may show a degree of subservience, even while he may be abusing her. This shadowed area of the interaction of Black and white minds is too complex to be explained away in simple equations. It belongs to that field so well explored by Frantz Fanon, "The Psychology of the Oppressed". The whole fibre of Black life has been permeated and poisoned by white values and oppression in such a way that many Black people cannot live comfortably with themselves. They have a devouring sense of alienation within. They judge themselves by white standards even while they fight for Black identity.

Take the example of the definition of female beauty. Since the days of slavery, our idea of what constitutes attractiveness was governed by the ideal represented by the slavemaster's wife, with her pale colouring, her straight nose, her blue eyes, her thin lips, her artifically induced slenderness. We forgot our admiration of the various shades of skin colour, back in Africa, where the very darkest were traditionally idealized, being compared to smooth black pebbles on the seashore or to the darkest myrtle fruit. A round healthy figure was preferable to the willowy look of a slim woman; the rounded backside was better than the flat, typically European shape; full lips were more desirable than the thin, sometimes lipless mouths of many white people. Yet today our young people are often confused about the standards to which to aspire. To many of them, long hair has become the most desirable feature of female beauty, to the extent that some girls do everything to stretch their own, or "relax" it, so as to approximate to the white ideal.

Where white values are the ideal, many young Black people suffer a crisis of identity. Society in some ways validates the white bias, for people of mixed race are often the first to benefit when political pressures force various bodies and institutions to take on the Black unemployed. Throughout our Black history we witness the attempt by white societies in different parts of the world to create divisions among Black people, the readiness to mete out unequal treatment to Black people of mixed race as against Black Blacks. They did it with the so-called Mulattoes of the Carribean and the Americas, the house slaves and the field slaves. They did it with the so-called Coloureds of South Africa. And we can see the old practice rearing its ugly head in our community here. They create small privileges, and work opportunities which help to divide our Black communities into the haves and the have-nots. If the practice persists we shall soon have our own racial and class divisions to struggle against.

So the image is confirmed that nothing succeeds like whiteness. The agony of the young Black person who tries in vain to change in order to be acceptable can be imagined. Blackwomen are struggling to validate Black images, to project a new self-acceptance and appreciation of our looks. But we are up against the engulfing society, bolstered as it is by the media. Those of mixed parentage are in an even more unenviable position for, while they could identify with either community, racism militates against them. They may want to outgrow the image of the "tragic mulatto" yet have to deal with white rejection and the prevailing attitudes towards Blackness. Instead of being drawn to identifying with either half of themselves, they are often pushed one way or another or else repelled both ways. The choice to be Black and accepted as such by other Black people has to be an emphatic one. They have to live demonstrably Black lives and make a conscious decision to renounce their white heritage.

Maud Sulter has written explicitly about these problems and the choices that have to be made – an affirmation that resounds the more loudly from someone who has been in this invidious position. She guards her Blackness jealously, perhaps aggressively, with a defiance of tone that is sometimes akin to bitterness. Her poems "My Blackness, My Cloak" and "Jacaranda" explore a recurring theme among Blackwomen. Marsha Prescod writes similarly. There is distrust of those white "trendies" who, while most people are struggling up the mobility ladder, straining upwards in society, go "down" to the black ghettos, to "our" Brixton, as they would to a theatrical performance. To them we are quaint, novel, exotic – anything

but real. "They pilfer our Culture, our foods and our sounds."
They seek to impose their ideas and their stereotypes on our
reality, expecting us to join in their games. We share the status
of animals at the zoo. Needless to say, this is hurtful and we do
not welcome that kind of solidarity. On the other hand, there is
a silent recognition between any two Blacks, especially where
they find themselves in isolation, lost among white crowds.
Maud Sulter pursues this thought in her poem "If Leaving
You": a Black stranger is not altogether a stranger because
Blackness itself is the bond between them, even before they
encounter one another.

This introduction covers in broad outline the experiences of
Blackwomen in Britain today which are the cornerstone of our
writing. It attempts to explore on the one hand the social,
political and economic factors, and, on the other, questions of
race, gender and class. These influence our lives, our views and
our literature in the 1980s. A literary contribution is vital to the
development of any culture, for it is the embodiment of a
people's heritage. In it is coded the compressed experience of
the whole society, its beliefs, its progress and its values; in short,
the universal truth. And where social forces splinter society into
cultural enclaves, it is essential that all facets of reality are
reflected in the universal truth.

British society today is splintered and categorized in many
varied ways. Not too long ago, there was no such identifiable
thing as the Blackwoman's viewpoint; but now there is. Much
as we regret the splintering of the national experience into theirs
and ours, Black and white, male and female, the reality forces
us to recognize and accept it as such. Relegating our writing to a
separate category, the "Black and female" genre, is actually
doing us some good after all.

From now on we exist. Where we had no collective considered viewpoint, now we have. In books such as this, we are
carving for all Blackwomen a niche in British society.

Needless to say, the critical opinions expressed in this introduction are my own. They are not necessarily shared by the
women writers who have contributed to this volume.

AMRYL JOHNSON

Amryl Johnson was born in Trinidad, West Indies, and came to England at the age of eleven. Her education continued at schools in London and at the University of Kent, where she completed a degree in African and Caribbean studies.

Her collection of poems *Long Road to Nowhere* was published by Virago Press in 1985. Her poetry appears in the following anthologies: *News for Babylon* (Chatto & Windus, 1983), *Facing the Sea* (Heinemann, 1986), *With a Poet's Eye* (Tate Gallery Publications, 1986), and *Watchers and Seekers* (The Women's Press, 1987). A poet on the "Writers in Schools" circuit, she has broadcast on radio in this country as well as the Caribbean and has read her work extensively.

She has recently published *Sequins for a Ragged Hem* (Virago, 1988), her account of her return to the Caribbean in 1983. She is currently working on a collection of short stories set in the Caribbean and hopes to complete her first novel before returning to the islands in 1988 to continue her travels. She lives in Coventry.

*   *   *

The crunch came about eight years ago.

The novel I was working on demanded a great deal of research into slavery. It seemed as if every book I read simply went further and further into individual cases of brutality. Unbelievable. It was impossible to separate the facts from the emotion. I became very morose, very depressed and bitter. Out of this period came the poem "Midnight Without Pity" (1977):

Judas,
       take my hand
let us go from here
down into the valley
Keep your hood tight
about your neck
I do not want to see
your face
and if you still remember
the bitter taste
to know
you never stood a chance
           or had a choice
against a destiny
  which held you
manipulated you
      rejected you
then teach me
      teach me
      teach me how
to count the silver
and forget the cost
for I am
Black
And I am
Angry
my name
is
Midnight
Without
Pity

A publisher who read some of my early poems said, "I would like to take on your work but how do I market it? It is like a scream of rage. How do I publish a scream of rage?" Maybe she had a point. I am not entirely convinced. The fact remains that I am writing about a period when, in the main, either Black writers in this country were not taken seriously or else publishers were afraid of what we had to say. There was no place for us on their lists.

Nevertheless, I can see how I am now able to do what seemed impossible at the time; harness and control the anger. The novel was completed. It was rejected, rejected and rejected again. Now it holds space in a dusty cupboard. It was suggested recently that I should rewrite it. I may do so one day. At present, it is too reminiscent of a time when I was porous to every whim of pain. The anger reigned like a tight fist and everything in the novel radiates from that well.

When you move on, you take the threads with you, blend them with the newer experience to weave a different tapestry.

The crunch came eight years ago but I had been writing long before then. Words had always fascinated me. Being able to translate an idea into written form has preoccupied me since childhood. The first tentative steps, apart from short stories and a little poetry written in the classroom, came during my early teens. The independent thought took a hammering. A number of unfinished stories bore testimony to this. The urge to write became a compulsion. That first novel took years to complete. I understand now about the growing process of my art. At the time, I was just beginning to walk, only I did not know it. The frustration had me writing and rewriting the same passage in order to find the words which wholly expressed what I was trying to say. Sentences were stilted and clumsy. The flow wasn't there. I don't know what happened to that book. I put it in the attic along with other early attempts. It may still have been there when my parents sold the house.

At the time I was in conflict. I seemed to be struggling with some decision as to whether I was first of all an individual and then a Black female or if the colour of my skin should influence every waking decision. I was in danger of loss of identity, struggling to emerge as a person beyond any bars or fetters which would hold me back. Or so it seemed. I believe my early writing reflected this dilemma.

I did not know I was in exile until a Trinidadian friend said, "Girl, you must go home. You must go home." This was in 1979. My parents had long since returned. I came to Britain to join them when I was eleven and, apart from two school-holiday visits when

I was twelve and sixteen, I had not returned. While being aware that I was a long way away from my island of origin, it had not occurred to me to go back there. It took three years before I made the trip. In short, I was afraid. Had I been away too long?

I went, and I stayed seven weeks. My fears were largely unjustified. It whetted my appetite sufficiently for me to take the opportunity when it arose the following year, 1983, to make a return visit. That trip lasted for six months. It started in the January before I was due to begin Part II of a degree in African and Caribbean Studies at the University of Kent. My travels took me from Trinidad and Tobago to Grenada, Barbados, St Lucia, Dominica, Guadeloupe and then back to Trinidad. The collection of poems *Long Road to Nowhere*, (Virago Press, 1985) was inspired by these months spent on the islands.

The Caribbean isn't all exotic fruit, white sands and coconut palms against a blue sky. The gulf between those who have and those who do not is too blatant to be ignored.

> Whitewash the face of hunger
> When all the features have been removed
> paint on the smile, the laughing eyes
> Show the tourists what they want
> But not too close
> Behind the grinning façade are slums
> which rob the people of all dignity
>
> ("Blowing in a Random Breeze",
> *Long Road to Nowhere*)

But I was also celebrating the rediscovery of my own culture. The Carnival poems affirm this. In merging the calypso beat with the island's dialect, I acknowledge this total acceptance.

> Dis abandon to pleasure is drawin' we
> to one conclusion of unity
> Freedom was bought wit' dis in min'
> a full expression ah liberty

> dey cahn take dis from we
> J'Ouvert is "we ting"

> ("J'Ouvert (We Ting)", *Long Road to Nowhere*)

Some critics failed to understand the significance of the title of my book. It relates to the stab of realization which caused me to describe the collection as a journey into awareness with a sting in the tail. The road that for six months took me to the Caribbean islands is the same road which brought me back to Britain to face what I have described as "a stranded horror". The incident shattered what I felt I had achieved. The journey would need to begin again, towards this new awareness. Therefore the road begins right here and now. At whichever point in time I find myself having to come to terms with something which takes me to the limit, traps me in my own footsteps, I must go back to reassess the journey.

> always
> the road
> crossed the road
> to the other side
> Walking up
> Waking up
> Open your eyes, lady
> and look
> Open your eyes you
> complacent
> superior
> bitch
> and look
> see where the road leads
> See where the road leads?

> ("Long Road to Nowhere",
>   *Long Road to Nowhere*)

The book I have just completed tells the story of the islands and the people of the Caribbean as I saw them during those six months. It is not a travelogue but a deeper look at life in the Lesser Antilles, the side which is inaccessible to white tourists. I sought to record the humour, the tragedies, the ironies, all those little touches which are peculiar to the islands and which make the Caribbean people so unique.

When did things start moving? It began with two readings in Oxford, my home town for some years now. After that, I suddenly found myself reading with well-known poets. That was in 1981. I was also doing some considerable amount of work in schools on the "Writers in Schools" circuit. In 1983, it snowballed. Everything started happening at once. I came back from the West Indies to find that the Chatto & Windus anthology of Black-British poetry *News For Babylon* was about to get off the ground. I received a letter from James Berry, the editor, asking me to contribute. Five of my poems are included in the anthology. A few months later, Virago Press rang to say they had seen my work, liked it and wanted to bring out a collection of my poetry. It really was as simple as that.

One journalist, while interviewing me, said she found all my work political. That came as quite a surprise. I would by no means use the word "political" to describe *all* my work. I can see the direction my work has been taking from the late 1970s. I do not set out to be overtly political. But I am motivated by an emotion so strong that some poems were penned in blood and tears. This one was written after a conversation with some people who felt that because I am a West Indian I could not fully understand the horror of South Africa:

> to the shadows
> I am shielded
> by circumstances
> But he
> and I
> are one
> Chained
> by the link
> which binds us

HE
   IS
      MY
         BROTHER!
His
SWEAT
are my
      tears

("He is my Brother")

Some of my most poignant poems were written around the same time. Nineteen eighty-one was crucifying. It was the year of the New Cross massacre. I also lost two young friends. "Shackles" came from that period. My preoccupation is a blatantly obvious one:

Shackled dead
in my tracks
catapulted back
in time
to taste
the icy thorns
of sorrow
Sent me stumbling
like a lunatic
to a bar
      Drink up!
the man said
      It's closing time!
I choke
on the dregs
of my ancestry

("Shackles")

It was mortifying to be walking through an evening like any other autumn evening and suddenly find myself hurled into the experience described above. I am saying what I said in "He is my brother": "I cannot turn my back on this. It is too vital to be ignored."

Some of these early poems were brought out in a booklet (now out of print) by me. I did not approach any publishing house because I knew exactly the sort of format I wanted and was not going to be thwarted. Dark brown ink on fawn quality paper and several illustrations is not many publishers' idea of economy. All the typesetting and illustrations were done free of charge by friends in the business. The booklet proved to be an economic success. Why did I bring it out? I would find myself clutching corners of the room after a reading where my fellow poets would be kept busy signing copies of their books. Also, there always seemed to be someone present who liked my work enough to ask when I planned on bringing out a collection. I did it for them as much as myself. It was not a money-making venture. All I had to pay for was the printing and I sold copies at a pound each. I barely broke even. At the time the presentation seemed just as important as the poems. Bringing out that slim volume was a satisfying experience. I would encourage any young poets who wanted to bring out inexpensive publications (even photocopies!) of their work to do so.

Writing has become the most important thing in my life. No matter how marvellous the current man happens to be, if I cannot spend a little time every day developing my creative strands, I am frustrated. My day begins at seven-thirty. Not as impressive as it may sound: I do not sit down to the typewriter for another four hours. An early riser but a slow starter. Almost mechanically, I go through the motions of taking a bath, doing the washing up and all the other chores I feel I must first complete. Almost mechanically because all the while my brain is ticking over, shaping the day's work. When I sit down, I already have a reasonably clear idea of what I want to accomplish over the next few hours. The routine is an obvious one. Yet I regard myself as being undisciplined. I envy those writers who can sit for hours just burning up a hot typewriter. My hours are punctuated by innumerable trips for tea, coffee and sandwiches. I can take the threads to the kitchen with me and return in the same state of trance to continue from where I left off. I can take a phone call, chatting about this and that, and it will not annihilate my concentration. Starting the day before eight o'clock means that by mid-afternoon I am beginning to wilt. The ideas will continue turning over while I am lying down. If I am able to fall asleep, it will only be for a little while. Either way, my working day continues like this until eight or nine o'clock.

I worked for an employment agency while writing the second novel. Temping for them meant I would take nine-to-five employment two to three weeks at a time to earn enough money so I could spend the next two to three weeks writing. I live economically so this worked quite well. Nowadays, I can support myself by giving readings, taking workshops and creative writing sessions in schools. I will soon be taking on a post as Writer in Residence attached to an East Midlands college and I look forward to the opportunity it will offer to broaden my horizons. Another category of writers I admire are those who can hold down a nine-to-five job permanently and devote their evenings to their craft. I fear I may not be made of such stern stuff.

I did the framework for a number of the poems in *Long Road to Nowhere* while I was in the Caribbean. The outline for others was only in my head. Almost the entire collection was completed during the 1984 summer vacation and largely during the month of August. I was housekeeping for one of the lecturers on campus while he and his family were on holiday. Glorious isolation! A large house and a private, spacious garden. I was one of the few people who didn't go home that summer. It was just myself and the family cat — a little bit of company for when I started to feel the pinch. During that month I lived in a strange world, far more intense than anything I had ever experienced before. The ideas flowed and flowed and flowed. Each thought was like a tidal wave, stronger than the last. They took me down. I ate, slept, I lived poetry. Lost in the realms of creativity, forms I had never before experimented with came easily to the fore. It was also the first time I had attempted to write in creole. I took the step confidently. Ideas came visually. Image after image was evoked like scenes running through my head. I had only to capture the moments and translate them into the appropriate form:

Yuh fresh fish?

Woman, why yuh holdin' meh fish up tuh yuh nose?
De fish fresh. Ah say it fresh. A ehn go say it any mo'

Hmmm, well if dis fish fresh den is I who dead an' gone
De ting smell like it take a bath in a lavatory in town
It here so long it happy. Look how de mout' laughin' at we
De eye turn up to heaven like it want tuh know 'e fate
Dey say it does take a good week before dey reach dat state
("Granny in de Market Place" 1985,
Long Road to Nowhere)

If people find, as a number of them have said, that the poem really
comes alive for them then they have the Muse to thank for
bringing this grandmother figure so vividly to my mind.

When writing prose, I go straight to the typewriter. With
poetry, I work in pencil. I may need to go to a third draft before I
achieve what I set out to. Only the poet knows when it is finished.
I have up to a dozen poems which by other people's standards are
completed. By my own, they are not. They may remain
unfinished. I may never find exactly what I am looking for. It is
all very well for the critics to write as if they are authorities on
your work, criticizing your imagery for not being concise,
inconsistencies in the standard of your work, etc. What comes
over a lot of the time is that they do not even understand what you
are trying to say. This is the annoying part. In some cases, they do
not even come *close* to comprehending. It comes as quite a shock
to read an article sounding off about the inappropriate title of the
collection. The person then goes on to give the reason. He hasn't
interviewed you. He has never met you in his life yet has the
audacity to act as if he can get inside your head. He *knows* what
you were thinking. What's more, you can tell by his well-worn
choice of phrases that he hasn't even read them carefully. The
Virago collection was well reviewed. I gave up after reading the
third review. It became too painful an exercise.

Earlier, I wrote about having to go to three drafts on some of
the *Long Road to Nowhere* collection. There is one poem which
I completed on my first effort: the title poem. I put it off for as

long as I could. Having to lay that ghost would be an extremely painful experience. I sat down in the remotest corner of the garden, the cat purring at my elbow, and picked up the notebook and pencil. This was going to be different. I was on my own. No Muse, no cocoon of creativity could help me here. This was too stark and raw. I would need to relive the experience, retrace my footsteps. I had the idea of a form far simpler, words less torrid than what came. It came like a vomit, in a torrent of uncontrollable tears. Blood and tears, all over again. And like those early poems, once finished I could not go back to them. They said everything I wanted to say, everything I needed to say. And the form was perfect. It *was* the road.

If there was such a thing as a centrally heated garden, it would be my ideal year round environment in which to write. The cat is no problem. Midnight, our cat here in Oxford, is never far away. Whether I am working in the garden or indoors, she provides wonderful company and inspiration. I would recommend a cat's company to any writer who prefers not to work in complete isolation.

Future plans? Another volume of poetry and a book on childhood in the Caribbean, I am just sharpening my pencil and oiling my typewriter to get down to them. I often work simultaneously. Well, *almost* simultaneously!

Amryl Johnson, 1985

JULIE PEARN ON AMRYL JOHNSON

After more than three decades during which almost all the (published) black writers in Britain have been men, the black women writers who have recently emerged so vibrantly have done much to broaden and deepen the scope of the literature. The male writers have, quite legitimately, tended to concentrate on immediate struggles within the society. In the work of Joan Riley, Grace Nichols and in the *Motherland* project, we see these immediate struggles placed in the context of an overarching desire for historical reconstruction, for re-establishing the continuities of a twice-dispossessed people. Amryl Johnson's work makes an important contribution to this process of rebuilding the shattered fragments.

Amryl's earlier poems are full of a sense of bleakness and cold which is spiritual as much as physical. The British environment offers her images of thorns, dead leaves and brackish waters. These are not abstract images but reflect the hostility she feels from the society towards herself and all black people, and a general absence of love and creativity. Feelings of grief, pain, insecurity and panic are pervasive:

> There is a ring of rusty iron
> which grates along concrete
> until your blood crawls
> ("Circle of Thorns")

Such feelings are rooted in the actual experience of black people, both historical and contemporary.

She describes vividly the sense of having no control over one's destiny. A short story, "Marcus", portrays a young black boy caught up in an endless nightmare against the barriers of the "straight" world around him:

> Walls are walls. Bars are bars. By the time he was twelve, Marcus's eyes were like whirlpools mirroring whirlpools. His head, turning in slow circles, followed the thin coil of destiny spiralling steadily upwards to engulf him.

Marcus's endeavours to break the spiral and join the "straight" world are full of the most acute ironies.

A poem, "Another Stab at the Wishing Well" (the word "stab" again evokes harshness and insecurity), has the author longing for firm-rooted safety and protection from "the whips and daggers/which flay me with impunity":

> I wish
> I was hard and sturdy
> like a rock set deep in the ocean

Then, she says, lulled by the waves, she would sleep forever. While content with the prospect of unconsciousness, she hints her knowledge that this is not enough, that she will be simply "Oblivious to ruin".

Her return to the Caribbean makes a breakthrough as clearly personal as it is professional. It has enabled her to confront literally, and frequently demolish, fears and pain which had previously emerged as a generalized sense of horror in her poetry:

> . . . those emaciated spectres
> which rise from the trenches of near
> forgotten battles
> hungry for recognition
> ("How Do You Feed the Ghosts?",
> *Long Road to Nowhere*)

Her physical journey was also a journey to self-knowledge as a woman with Caribbean and African roots. Located in the West Indies itself, the horror takes on more sharply defined images of slavery, with which gradually the writer comes to identify herself:

> New found courage to turn from the power of
> its glare habit of obedience and look at
> yourself without feeling shame you start
>   coming to face the mirror
> still   coming
>   coming
>
> ("Far Cry",
> *Long Road to Nowhere*)

Significantly, the poem begins by talking about "they", shifts partway to "you", which identifies the writer with the Caribbean people around her and mutual African ancestors "coming to build your own foundations", and ends with "she", the writer. The "only one" who "finds herself".

Journeys are not only related to self-discovery. They have been, historically, related to the uprooting of communities, dispossession, slavery and migration. Amryl describes her recognition of this in "The New Cargo Ship", which on one level describes a voyage of Trinidadian tourists to the neighbouring island of Tobago. Now radios blare "on the sea/once their enemy". Yet the thought going through the writer's head at the sight of black people crammed on a boat distances her from all the others who are, to all appearances, simply having a good time:

> And where was I in all this?

In the Caribbean, the writer is faced with a paradox. On one hand, she has never felt more whole, and has her identity affirmed by everything which surrounds her; on the other, she recognizes that her years in Britain have brought other dimensions which isolate her. The recognition comes with humour and appreciation for what she has missed. Her participation in the Trinidad Carnival is not merely a cultural experience, it is "a lesson in living". Witnessing the steel bands' Panorama is for the crowd a rich, uninhibited experience of food, drink, reunion and cultural celebration. The poet is drawn admiringly into this vortex of energy before suddenly stepping back, with ironic detachment:

> I am humbled by their generosity
> I am dwarfed by their magnanimity
> I am envious of their spontaneity
> I am —
> Am I the only person looking at the band?
> ("Panorama from the North Stand",
> *Long Road to Nowhere*)

What she admires most is that the responses are so genuine and total. When Catelli All Stars are playing, "enthusiasm knows no bounds", but when the legendary Desperadoes take the stage, the response is indifferent. The poet is "Dumbfounded" and asks what is going on. All is explained by the reply: "We eh like dat tune!" At this moment she expresses her deepest joy in her heritage:

> My people are like the leaves of an evergreen
> planted in the finest dawn

Her joy in the richness of imagery which comes so naturally in the course of Trinidadian talk is nowhere so evident as in her delightful and funny "Granny in de Market Place", where she captures a rhythm of confrontational exchange between customer and stallholders:

> Yuh mango ripe?
>
> Gran'ma, stop feelin' and squeezin' up meh fruit!
> Yuh ehn playin' in no ban'. Meh mango eh no concertina
>
> Ah tell yuh dis mango hard just like yuh face.

The contrast between the imagery drawn from the Caribbean and from Britain could not be more stark. "Nutmeg" is one of Amryl's most perfect poems, working into the lifecycle of the nutmeg, the growing stages of female sexuality from the virgin "perfect/peach" to procreation:

> Spent
> but not discarded
> Your empty womb
> a shell which
> bears the fragrance
> the perfumes
> of your labour

The emphasis is on life-abundance, not sterility and paralysis.

The issue of control over one's destiny re-emerges. In "The Loaded Dice", the poet uses the vivid context of a dice-throwing fortune-telling game to reflect on the arbitrary nature of the African's fate at the hands of Europeans: the carve-up of the continent, the "legacy to pass from han' to han'". Participation in the dice-game implies an acceptance of powerlessness, of an arbitrary destiny. Though constantly commanded to "Throw de dice, girl, throw!" her fingers freeze and finally refuse in a militant assertion that it is possible to change the course of history:

> We hah to fin' de will to free weself
> Leave de pas' behind, it dead an' gone but
> let de memory give we de strength to push
> fuh what we want

Linking the continents in struggle, she asserts the necessity to fight "fuh we rights":

> Is bottle, stick and brick fuh some ah we
> Gun an' tank fuh we sister an' we brudder
> in other countries

Some of this new conviction may have come from her visit to Grenada where, she says, the vision of "Spices and Guns" did nothing to disturb her "concepts of what/ is right or what is wrong".

She learns something of what Europe has done to her personality; there is a bit of the imperialist in her too. In "The Birds Must East Also", she portrays herself so eager for the fruits of "paradise" that she tears at the branches, throws stones at what she cannot reach. In her ecstasy of reunion, she has to be reminded of the things she "forgot/ to remember":

> " — at the very least
> the birds must eat also"

White friends are another undeniable part of her. "Tread Carefully in Paradise" expresses sadness for the pain which white visiting friends, innocent of the Caribbean's brutal past, are made to sffer as walking symbols of imperialism. She absolves them as blameless, yet cannot blame their attackers. She blames herself for allowing them to come unarmed with greater understanding. She takes on board the delicate responsibility of teaching them the enormity of mutual history:

> to try and make them comprehend
> why their ordeal can never count
> for any more than just
> one grain of sand

The return to Britain represented, initially at least, a return to nightmare; the end of a long road to nowhere. A damaged black man crosses and recrosses London's Kentish Town Road:

> his eyes
> caged
> trapped at the zebra
> ("Long Road to Nowhere",
> > *Long Road to Nowhere*)

She feels the cruel mockery of white bystanders as the poor man's behaviour confirms for them the myth which fuels their racism:

> gorilla on a zebra's back
> the myth which makes
> them smile
> hide their mouths
> behind their hands

Before her journey to the Caribbean she might not have been able to bear the shame of being identified with this man. Now she recognizes that his cage is hers also:

> I carry him on
> my back

Her allegiances are firmly formed: she and he together face a hostile, racist world. And, she says:

> this gun
> looking at them
> will serve
> us
> both

In her poems, Amryl expresses emotion with a tough frankness. Her descriptions of grief suggest an intimate acquaintance. She uses images to convey feelings otherwise indescribable:

> and my last words are impaled
> on that thorn-racked hedge
> ("The Unpaved Road")

This comes from a portrayal of a parting from a beloved person with whom things have gone irredeemably wrong. The pain is rendered more, not less, acute by the poet's refusal to "make waves". Quite naturally, this extends to an image of drowning as she "goes down":

> tight-lipped and reticent
> hanging on with fists of steel
> like any marooned slave
> clinging to the wreckage

Her image of the "marooned slave" suggests two meanings simultaneously: one, being washed up, with little or nothing; the other, fighting fiercely from the hinterland for independence (reinforced by the "fists of steel"). Together they vividly convey the strength of a woman fighting for survival without any of the props of status: wealth, race or gender. Amryl has been an example to me of the most tremendous singlemindedness. There was a time when she was prepared to go without everything just in order that she might write. The emergence of her work is testimony to the resilience of a courageous black woman.

MAUD SULTER

Maud Sulter is a journalist who also writes poetry and fiction. Her first collection, *As A Black Woman*, was published by Akira Press in 1985. Her work has appeared in various books and also in magazines such as *Spare Rib*. Her poetry is included in *Dancing the Tightrope* and *Watchers and Seekers*, both published by The Women's Press in 1987. Other entries include *Through the Break* (prose) and *Charting the Journey* (in conversation with Alice Walker), both with Sheba Feminist Publishers, 1987.

* * *

NOTES OF A NATIVE DAUGHTER

Being black has never been a problem for me. Thankfully I have never sat in a bathtub scouring my skin to make it white, doubted that Africa was my spiritual homeland, or fallen into the cultural void that would demand the denial of the myriad experiences and facets of my life in the name of assimilation. No. Being black is not a problem. The problem lies in the threatening racism, institutionalized and individual which seeks to destroy black people not only within larger white communities such as Britain or the USA but globally as well.

As a blackwoman writer, my adventures with the written word began when I was three. Measles had put me to bed and I was bored (a dangerous situation that still threatens me more than poverty, sickness or rejection — more of which later). Anyway, in the course of events I learnt to write my name and there was no stopping me after that. Another childhood skill was the ability to memorize stories. Much to the amazement of a cousin, I recited the whole of *Pussykins* and *Puppykins*. She couldn't believe that I wasn't reading it from the page and I couldn't believe it was any big deal. My grandfather took care of my daily well-being while my mother took care of putting food on the table, clothes on my back and paying the rent.

Grandad and I indulged ourselves in writing sessions at the kitchen table. My grandfather obviously had lots of stories to tell me which he knew I was too young to fully understand. Sadly, cancer was taking control in his eighty-year-old frame. So he wrote me his story, his likes and dislikes — music, performers, politicians, and poetry. I still have it and would like to see it published as a cultural rebellion — White working-class creativity and experience told, not as a sociological study written by some middle-class academic, but from the horse's mouth, so to speak.

During the traumatic times following his death I would seek solace in looking at the beautiful handwritten script and try to make communion with his spirit. One poem in particular helped me to maintain my self-respect as a little black girl growing up in Glasgow in the late 1960s, to mid-1970s.

TO MY GRAND-DAUGHTER ON HER FOURTH BIRTHDAY

> My Darling Has a Heart of Gold
> Although she's only four years old
> Her teeth are white, they look like pearls
> Her jet black hair, a mass of curls.
>
> Her lips are red they look so sweet
> Her eyes are brown she looks a treat.
>
> I love her dearly, she loves me
> I wouldn't swop her for China's tea
> Or the coffee in Brazil.
>
> Her smiles are sweet
> They catch the eye
> Of people who are passing by.
>
> She looks so fit so very neat
> She's so attractive & so sweet.

My Days Have Not Been Quite So Lonely
Since she became my one and only.

WGS

Twenty years later I was to dedicate my first published collection of poetry, *As a Blackwoman*, to him. It was the centenary of his birth. The following poem introduces my work within the context of my childhood experiences.

HEADSTONE

An unmarked grave
for the person who
was closest to
my childhood.

This reality has haunted me
for sixteen long years

Headstones cost money
and money was short.

Single parenthood
for the workingclasses
in the 60's
bears no resemblance
to the *alternative living*
of the *progressive
upwardly mobile*
woman of today

One day I shall carve
for you a stone

Etched with the words
you taught me to express

But until then
I shall keep you
here with me
in my soul.

After the 1984 Vera Bell Prize was won by the collection's title poem "As a Blackwoman", Desmond Johnson from Akira Press approached me, asking if I had more work with a view to publication. I had already approached Virago but they had postponed their decision about who to include in their poets series because they said Maya Angelou, the black American writer, wanted them to publish her poetry as they publish her prose. So, as a bird in the hand is worth two in the bush, I decided to support a young black press rather than take the work to one of the other more established poetry publishers.

As seems to be the case across the board for blackwomen endeavouring to have their work published, I ran into problems. My suggestions for cover artists, drawn from three years' research into black and Asian women's creativity in Britain and direct experience in publishing, were dismissed and the book was published with stereotyped images of "Blackwomanhood" drawn by a man. I sought solace in the fact that Alice Walker still has problems with her covers after nearly twenty years of being published.

Three incidents influenced my decision to publish poetry. A writing week at the Arvon Foundation in Yorkshire held in the spring of 1984. Grace Nichols the poet and Caryl Phillips the playwright were our resident writers. The course was for blackpeople — a tremendous success, and a turning point in my writing. Unfortunately, the Arvon Foundation did not see fit to repeat the course in 1985. As blackpeople we had many different experiences and conceptualizations of our African roots. For myself, it inspired me to write fiction and poetry and use these forms as a means to express my experiences as a blackwoman born and brought up in Britain. On my return to London I entered *As A Blackwoman* in the Black Penmanship (sic) Awards competition. Which brings us back to Desmond Johnson's support.

Before moving on, there is one more poem in the collection which it would be useful to look at here — "Thirteen Stanzas". This poem was written shortly after the death of an older woman who had been a friend to me for nearly ten years. Her death brought home to me on an individual level the brutality of hysterectomy within the "health" service. It is written in the phonetic style of the tongue of the city of my birth. Although I was highly skilled in the use of standard (whose?) English, it took considerable forethought to present an understandable system within which to present this highly emotional and deeply felt poem. Here are the first, fourth and fifth stanzas as an introduction to the style:

> trips tae the local. shoapin centre.dogshit.boarded up
>   businesses.
> capital before people.profit before
>   need.hustle.bustle.cheery *hullos.*
> *how's it gawin?.how ra wains?.n the damp?.* auld school

> up tae the shoaps.in the past.a'd look forward.tae
>   seein.that tall gaunt
> figure.appear.running fae hir hoose.tae hir mithers.the
>   fishvan.tae the
> butchers.never too busy.to stoap fur a chat.a natter.a
>   rap.steamin hoat

> tea/in the bakers.sit doon.roll n sausage.a confectioners
>   nightmare.
> bilious.mysteriously hued.sugar fuels hollow bellys.we
>   remember hunger.or.
> the hunger of others.talk o the family.the new kids.the
>   strikes.lay offs.

I write from deeply felt experience and I believe that my poetry will continue to develop if I do, as it expresses my more deeply experienced emotions. Love and the blues are presenting themselves as the themes of the next collection. The question of who will publish it is anybody's guess.

Some of my deepest feelings relate to the question of racial harassment. My first taste of racism was in the language and behaviour of white children. As a child I was advised to respond along the lines of —

> 'sticks'n stones
> might break ma bones
> but words'll
> never hurt me.'

Given that the words "nigger", "paki", "darkie", invariably did hurt it seemed a bit stupid to say they didn't. However, since I was never physically beaten up, beyond the odd stone or spittle attempt, perhaps the adage served a purpose. And perhaps if there had been a blackperson around to sympathize and advise on the situation, having experienced it themselves, times might have been less alienating. Only twice did I retaliate physically.

When I was fourteen I came face to face with a wider reality. Here James Baldwin, whom I wish I could have read in secondary school, points to the sickness that imposes itself on the thinking blackperson in the diaspora.

> *Once this disease is contracted, one can never be really carefree again, for the fever, without an instant's warning, can recur at any moment. It can wreck more important things than race relations. There is not a Negro alive who does not have this rage in his blood — one has the choice, merely, of living with it consciously or surrendering to it. As for me, this fever has recurred in me, and does, and will until the day I die.*
>
> (*Notes of a Native Son*, James Baldwin)

It was lunchtime. My friend and I had gone into a baker's to buy something for lunch. As we queued we were told to move along the counter. At the end of the counter were trays of uncovered food. We hesitated. The nasty evil white bitch (there I've said it after ten years; feminists will have to bear with me here — read on) told us again to move. Now being a well brought up Virgoan, I simply explained in a quiet voice that it would be unhygienic to stand over such openly displayed food. The incident was over in perhaps ten seconds but it took away a considerable part of my life. In the shop at the time there were administration workers from the school, other schoolkids and my closest competitor in our year whom I had known most of my life — male, blond and blue-eyed. And, of course, my best friend. I have replayed this scene in my mind hundreds of times. I believe that the speed with which the situation presented itself and the subtlety of the statement made it unlikely that anyone other than myself and my assailant were aware of what went on. The afternoon passed in a daze and how I got home I don't know, but the moment I turned the key in the door behind me I collapsed. I can see myself still crouched behind the door. Afraid but not sure why. There was no one I could talk to who could possibly understand what I was going through.

I had dismissed the racism of the children and others as simple ignorance. Grownups had been pretty good to me. So when I found myself confronted by the simple statement "I don't have to take that sort of talk from *you* people," I was confused and shattered. The implications were clear. Some adults believed in racial superiority. Whether I had heard Enoch Powell's "Rivers of Blood" speech I do not know. What I did know was that *these people* were the only half of *my people* that I knew. The implication was that I should go where I came from but I neither asked nor wanted to be there specifically, nor did I intend to go anywhere until I was ready. This woman, however, had obviously identified with the fascism of Powell and his ilk. So now my world seemed even more fragile than before.

My school work suffered and I spent month after month at home. Was the fear of confronting the world rational or irrational? Retreat into my self was the only way I knew to keep myself alive. That then became as pernicious as the disease itself. The only option left was flight. My dreams of a bright future died and psychiatry or law as careers were swept under the carpet. A fashion college in London offered me a place and I took it, not for the glamour of the course or the excitement of the metropolis, but simply to get myself moving again. An attempt to live again.

An incident ten years later, during the 1984 Edinburgh Festival, brought the situation into clearer focus. The Festival was privileged to have several Black American performers that year: Jessye Norman, Sweet Honey in the Rock and the Negro Ensemble Company. I had been invited to a party with the NEC administrator. It was on the other side of town so we queued for a cab in Waverley Station. Two homosexual men, about twenty-five years of age, were further back in the queue, regaled in the statutory clone gear of the time: suntan, blond tints, virile masculinity. Now I know that if they had come under attack while standing in that queue I would have gone to their aid, as I believe that oppression must be challenged on all levels. However, I began to feel threatened by their behaviour. Although they were jumping their place in the queue that in itself is not the most heinous crime in the world. What I realized, however, was that towards us, a blackwoman and a blackman, they were exhibiting real animosity. They were looking for a fight. Our individual sexuality was of no consequence to them. They wanted to attack us. Such incidents have taught me the penetrating bitterness of hate. Yes, there are times when hating is inescapable.

That scene has played itself out in my mind many times. Here I am reminded of James Baldwin again because these words made that situation and others much clearer to me. Having been refused service in a diner because they " . . . *don't serve Negroes here*", Baldwin went looking deliberately for the swankiest restaurant he could find. When again refused service, he threw a water pitcher at the waitress. The reality of the situation and its possibilities caught up with him and he made a run for it.

> *I lived it over and over and over again, the way one relives an automobile accident after it has happened and one finds oneself alone and safe. I could not get over two facts, both equally difficult for the imagination to grasp, and one was that I could have been murdered. But the other was that I had been ready to commit murder. I saw nothing very clearly but I did see this: that my life, my 'real' life, was in danger, and not from anything other people might do but from the hatred I carried in my own heart.*

> (*Notes of a Native Son*)

The tide of emotion that the incident triggered off was so violent and uncharacteristic that it worried me. I lay awake at night remembering two incidents as a child. In one a child called me a "black darkie" or something similar while I was walking with my mother. Out of embarrassment for her I grabbed him by the throat, held him against the wall and told him quite calmly that if he ever called me names in front of my mother again I would smash his head open. He was in no doubt that I meant it. I wonder if I did. On another occasion there was another little boy — perhaps the same one, I don't know — I caught him calling names up my close, i.e. at the back of the flats where I lived. As he ran past me on the stairs I put my foot out and he tripped. I wanted him to hurt himself badly, maybe even break his neck. The very instant I had done it I regretted it because I realized in that instant that he/they had succeeded in lowering me to their level. I had become as bad as they.

So when similar emotions were released at least fifteen years later, I had to reassess my position as a blackwoman in a hostile society. Part of that reassessment was a stronger commitment to my writing. Identifying with other black people's experience brought me relief. I was brought closer to them individually, collectively, politically, and I was no longer alone. I had a responsibility to help other black people realize the importance of their own experience and challenge that internalized (self) hatred that eats away at the soul. To bring self-expression to many black women living in Britain I have facilitated a number of writers' workshops, especially after the First International Feminist Bookfair in 1984.

Outside London the response is often more immediate. There is considerable energy and diversity of women's work throughout Great Britain, in cities like Liverpool, Bristol, Leicester, Cardiff and many other British towns. Blackwomen writers whose work ought to be taken more seriously, by the feminist publishers in particular, remain unpublished. The GLC (Greater London Council) and ILEA (Inner London Education Authority) funded the Women's Education Resource Centre where I carried out the Blackwomen's Creativity Project 1984–86 and sponsored a residential writing week for women of African and Asian descent in the summer of 1985 to coincide with the Edinburgh International Festival. It was a tremendous success. Women shared work, developed themes and most importantly networked to provide contacts for the future. There is a great diversity of work:

poetry, prose, journalism, criticism, plays for television and the stage together give an indication of the many fields in which women from those groups are working. Themes include child abuse, sexuality, culture and community life. This group represents just the tip of the iceberg. Our creativity is strong and constantly developing.

Having highlighted the importance of helping women get their writings down on paper or tape, the question of publication arises. That women write for themselves is vitally important on an individual level. Therefore, the problem of unpublished works should be recognized. Just because a piece of work is published should not necessarily give its ideas or themes more credence. However, in order to communicate with each other and the rest of the world, avenues of communication need to be sought.

In an article in the summer 1984 issue of *Artrage*, the intercultural arts magazine, I explored the problems of racism and our exclusion from and by the feminist publishing world. I pointed out that blackwomen have to contend with racism even in feminist books, and that we are concerned about the future of black British-based women writers. We are caught up in all kinds of contradictions.

Feminist Publishing

Introduction
The Feminist Book Fair of 1984 focused directly on our position here. From the start there had been a commitment to an international perspective. More than 16 countries were represented, including many from the black world — with participants from Zimbabwe, India, Malaysia and many others. Writers such as Audre Lorde (USA), Ellen Kuzwayo (South Africa) and Flora Nwapa (Nigeria) participated in readings, debates and talks. The Fair and associated events were bound to increase sales for the feminist presses and other commercial presses who were catching on to the lucrative market. Staging the event obviously helped women to fight their oppression under patriarchy but not the dynamics of race in contemporary feminist publishing. The issues of sex and race

go together. We have got to look into the question of racism in feminist books, which black women are being published, the future of black British-based women's writing and the contradictions between these facts.

Racism in books takes many forms. Books like *Union Street* by Pat Barker (Virago, 1982) reveal obvious direct racism; whereas *Sex and Love*, edited by Sue Cartledge and Joanna Ryan (The Women's Press, 1983), show their racism by exclusion. *Come Come* by Jo Jones (Sheba, 1983), and books like it show racism by misinterpretation.

Feminist Publishers

The boom in feminist publishing in Britain focuses around five major presses: Virago, The Women's Press, Pandora, Onlywomen and Sheba. All employ workers, predominantly white middle-class, bring books out regularly and keep their heads above water financially. Onlywomen and Sheba are independent self-funded presses not reliant on "Big Brothers" as the others are. For instance, Pandora is Routledge & Kegan Paul's feminist list and The Women's Press is backed by the Namara group. A review of their backlists illustrates not only specific racist content by white women writers but that the only blackwomen consistently published are AfroAmerican. This constitutes racism by the exclusion of the voices of Blackwomen in Britain and elsewhere.

Their forthcoming publications highlight a trend towards blackwomen's anthologies and the token inclusion of blackwomen in their generally white anthologies. In publishing, anthologies are cheap to produce. First, the publisher makes a one-off payment to the authors and invariably undercuts the royalties percentage within the budget. Secondly, little support by way of advances or re-writing is necessary. Thirdly, suddenly the House has published several blackwomen.

These adverse facts point to one great need — a Blackwomen's press in Britain and the importance of challenging the feminist presses while continuing to write.

Feminist Publishing

Liberating Ourselves

Blackwomen have the power to break the silence about our experience. Manuscripts need to be dusted down and sent to publishers. Others still need to be written. As always we need to be careful of tokenism. Rumour has it that a "white" anthology, i.e. with only a couple of black pieces, may be promoted on a fortnightly Black TV programme. Our commitment must be to blackwomen writers as a whole not the odd token gesture from white publishing houses.

And what of the presses? They need to prioritize the right of blackwomen to publish and edit books, get the books into libraries, keep the cover price as low as possible and keep the royalties figures as high as possible. Impossible? Nothing's impossible.

Part of the problem seems to lie in the definition of feminism/feminist practice itself. Black women have to consider how much a part of the feminist movement they are. This problem is not confined to Britain. Hence, for instance, American blackwoman writer Alice Walker has coined the term Womanist, to encompass our theories and practices which indeed historically are rooted well before the various periods of white feminism of the past two centuries. What perpetuates these problems is the reluctance of white society to acknowledge any permanence of black people on these shores. While the scale of immigration to Britain in the 1950s and 1960s from the Caribbean was significant in numerical terms, it must never be forgotten that there has been a black presence in Britain for at least the past four hundred years. Black communities such as those in Liverpool and Bristol date back hundreds of years. We are here, have been here for a long time and are here to stay. Yet our voices and histories are suppressed in order to maintain the lie that we are going back or will be sent back.

At present I am working on a play and a novel, in tandem with my academic work on Culture and Society. I have programmed this work to cover the next ten years. Living from hand to mouth makes establishing a secure home base difficult, and my work suffers.

Most importantly, within my work of this coming decade I hope to cultivate my African roots. Home is carried here with me in my heart. No one can ever take that away from me, although I anticipate that many will try.

Africa.   Pale Mother.   Roots.

I am I

See me
Perceive me

But I
Shall name

My self.

UNDER ATTACK

?ACT OF GOD

The stigmata on my thigh
appeared
not
by
divine
intervention
or
moral
reception

No

This eighth wonder of the world
owes
its
creation
to
violation

The oppression of one
black by another black
The subjection of one
woman by one man

God doesn't do his dirtywork himself
does he?
Men, who are the more deadly,
don't either

No

They bait you
then they mate you

Perfect you
then reject you

Rile you
then revile you

Choose you
then abuse you

No

The stigmata on my smooth
blackskinned thigh
appeared
not by divine
intervention
but
at the end
of a pair of
twelve inch shears

AS A BLACK WOMAN

As a blackwoman
the bearing of my child
is a political act.

I have
been mounted in rape
    bred from like cattle
    mined for my fecundity

I have
been denied abortion
    denied contraception
    denied my freedom to choose

I have
been subjected to abortion
    injected with contraception
    sterilised without my consent

I have
borne witness to the murders
of my children
by the Klan, the Front, the State

I have
borne sons hung for rape
for looking at a white girl

I have
borne daughters shot
for being liberationists

As a blackwoman
I have taken the power to choose
to bear a black child

— a political act?

As a blackwoman
every act is a personal act
every act is a political act

As a blackwoman
the personal is political
holds no empty rhetoric.

DOROTHEA SMARTT ON
MAUD SULTER

Maud Sulter is a multi-talented Blackwoman for whom I have a lot of admiration and respect. She was born and brought up in Scotland and now lives and works for Blackwomen's creativity. *As a Blackwoman* is her first published collection of poetry. The title is from her first published piece, which won the Vera Bell Prize in the 1984 Black Penmanship Awards. Most of her work was never intended for publication as she "scribbles" privately for release, which I have found many Blackwomen do. Her pieces can be very personal and overtly political. She moves from the "poetic" to the everyday in her style and content. Her work shows us our individuality, and the collectivity of our experience.

Her work is presented under seven different headings. The first, "Embrace", includes the title piece, a powerful testament to the abuse of our bodies, and our wombs. From rape and the contradictions of reproductive technology through to the pain that our mothers dealt with in a racist society, where our lives are always "disposable". In "Thirteen Stanzas" she again reminds us of this abuse of "medical practise medikill theory" with the loss of a friend and sister in struggle, through the control of women's sexuality. "Scots Triptych" is a piece consisting of three poems of love, desire and "treasuring the moment". I enjoyed these for their simplicity and their "romanticism". In "Passion Plays" Maud uses her incantations for/to African female spirits imbued with sexuality — Erzulie, Damballah, Aida Ouedo — to realize that passion. "Under Attack" is a theme that echoes in the poems under this heading, both from ourselves, for sometimes we can be our own worst enemies, and from the outside forces of repression and oppression. As Blackwomen we internalize a lot of anger, hatred and pain. Consequently depression or feeling suicidal can be a taken-for-granted feature of our lives. In her piece "Long Overdue", Sulter challenges the CND/Greenham concept of "peace", asking ". . . whose peace is it anyway?" where violence is a feature of our lives as Blackpeople locally and internationally — the violence of deprivation. In the poem "In the Ever Presence of the Enemy", I liked her challenging of categories and what it means to be a Blackwoman in this society. The poems in "I am an Artist" reaffirm just this. Blackwomen have been systematically denied access to this realm of themselves, or made to feel outside of its scope. It is important to our survival and sanity, and what it can mean for us — " . . . she is a lover and my only friend".

"Desertions" deals with loss and it expressed for me the vulnerability and sensitivity to living and loving. This section is made up of her shorter pieces which I felt were generally more effective. The heading "If" carries two of her longer pieces under it. "Winter Solstice" is addressed to the possibilities between Blackwomen and men, echoing our tradition of analysing our inter-relations and the sense of disappointment many of us have felt. "Empowerment" is a collection which reflects many things. It includes a celebration of our blackness and demands respect for that from particular sources:

MY BLACKNESS MY CLOAK

My blackness is a beautiful cloak
of selfhood that permeates my soul

So sister — white feminist

When you see
a bit of sun

Don't come
rushing to me

To say

"Look, I'll be as brown
(never black — god forbid)
as you soon"

or

also common

"I get even darker
than You"

Don't show
your peeling red flesh

Sister
I couldn't give a damn.

The poem "Jacaranda a café" — or rather its patrons — looks at a dangerous breed, "the downwardly mobile", and their attempts and collaboration in the attempt to stereotype us.

Maud's work speaks out against our stereotyping in general, but mainly in that our lives are not only a reaction to racism; we think and feel about all kinds of things. Like Maud, I feel that the cover drawing of her book is not a reflection of her work, and is itself now a cliché — however, the choice of artist was not hers. "As a Blackwoman" is the kind of poetry that grows on you with reading and re-reading and reflects a Blackwoman's experience with passion and sensitivity.

AGNES SAM

Agnes Sam is a South African of Indian descent now living in England. She was born in Port Elizabeth in the Eastern Cape. She read Zoology and Psychology at the Roman Catholic university in Lesotho, trained as a teacher in Zimbabwe, and worked in Zambia before realizing her interest in literature. She subsequently read English at York.

She has worked as a teacher, bank clerk, freelancer, secretary, cleaner, kitchen hand and has raised three sons. Her poetry and short fiction have been published in *Kunapipi* (Denmark), *The Story Must Be Told* (West Germany), and *Charting the Journey: Writings by Black and Third World Women* (eds. Shabnam Grewal *et. al.*), Sheba, 1988.

* * *

SOUTH AFRICA: GUEST OF HONOUR AMONGST THE UNINVITED NEWCOMERS TO ENGLAND'S GREAT TRADITION

South Africa occupies a place not to be envied with regard to her literature. On the one hand she poises, uncomfortably, in African literature: her discomfort caused by *our* knowledge that her internationally recognized writers are White. On the other, we occasionally see her artfully forcing her way in with Common-wealth literature in the unabashed manner of Israel's participation in the "Song for Europe" contest.

The dilemma of where to place South African writing is caused by an unusual response to her writers. While White South African writing is constantly placed before the reading public (through interviews and reviews for newspapers, magazines, radio and television, adaptations for film and sound, and distribution of books in shops, public and university libraries), Black South African writing poses an awkward problem for librarians, booksellers and teachers of literature. A walk around university and council libraries, chainstore and community bookshops provides evidence of the "guest of honour" and the "uninvited guest" handling of White and Black South African writers. Publishers have to be commended for the first. But what do we say to them about the second? Should the market for literature continue to be assessed on such obviously racial lines?

Virginia Woolf, writing in *A Room of One's Own* almost a century ago, suggests that the three factors which deter women from writing are a "lack of education", the "lack of access to publishing", and the "certainty that women would not make a living from writing". Have these deterrents been removed for women writers in the 1980s? For Black women writers? For the exiled Black woman writer?

Once we recognize that publishers believe the Black writer to be writing for Black readers, the question of earning a living from writing, a universal problem, is exacerbated for Black writers in exile. White South African writers who live and write in South Africa are guaranteed an audience there and here. Black South African writers who are in exile know that their works are not circulated in South Africa, and that any market basing itself on the Black reading public in England will restrict publications of their work. The situation of the Black South African woman *writing to earn a living in England* has never been touched upon by any discussion of women writers or African writers. Because it is the situation I am coping with, it is of concern to me.

I am an Indian and a Roman Catholic. These two facts were my passport out of South Africa and into Plus XII University College in Lesotho: there was no separate university for Indians when I matriculated, and the Separate Universities Bill was already in force.

At sixteen I travelled to Lesotho, then on to Zimbabwe, and finally to Zambia. These decisions were made without interference from my family, though they knew I'd be going to each of these countries without accompanying friends. The experience of

"Roma", in Lesotho, next to the freedom which the women and men in my family allowed my sisters and me, influenced my perspective of South Africa, and my attitude to male dominance. Ten years in independent Zambia added to what is now for me a matter of principle never to subscribe to the apartheid system by my mere presence there. Coming to England was a decision I opposed, but I was faced with the alternative of returning to South Africa — as a man's unaccompanied baggage?

In Zambia I'd been teaching and writing articles for young people intended to provide them with a background to African history before colonialism. The usual procedure for any teacher coming to Britain is to apply for qualified teacher status. The Department of Education and Science withheld this from me "for the time being", while granting it to some other South Africans. The effect on me was one of a tremendous loss of self-confidence.

Any woman forced to live in an environment where she is a foreigner, and then frustrated in her attempts to find employment, will find herself in the isolated world that leaves writing as her only option. Since she can't make a living in any other way, she will hope to make writing pay. Is it possible for a Black South African woman to make a living from writing in England in the 1980s?

At some stage I'd begun working on the "Bells" manuscript, but my situation was such that I had almost no contact with English-speaking people. My mother tongue, long since lost to me, isolated me from my community. Still entertaining hopes of teaching, it occurred to me that I had a Biology degree, and those teachers who were now actively teaching were Arts graduates, rather despised in Africa, but obviously thought highly of here. With this simplistic notion in my mind, I applied to the Universities Central Council for Admission to do a first degree in English.

At one university, I offered the rough draft of the "Bells" manuscript to be read before the interview in place of "recent essays". The interviewer made flattering comments, but if I expected to have to appear knowledgeable about any literary work or figure, I was to be disappointed. I was questioned at length about the arrangements I would make for my children, travelling in winter, how I would cope with a full-time course while caring for my children, and "Did I think that doing a degree was an easy thing?" It didn't require a supreme effort to realize that a man would never have been asked similar questions, and that my African degree counted for nothing.

At the second university the interviewer, confidently blunt, said, "The university will expect you to do A levels. After all you will be competing with English students who have just taken their A levels." In retrospect, I excuse these remarks with the hope that the interviewers may have neglected to read the UCCA form. At the time their remarks seemed so typical of what I had come to expect that I risked the offer of a place by responding with anger to both interviewers. I ended the second interview with the words, "I already have a university degree." Three universities made me unconditional offers.

At the university I chose to attend I faced three separate incidents of tutors not believing that the written work I was submitting was my own. *They* said this was because I rarely spoke during seminars and tutorials. *I* believe it was because criticism has become an area for arrogance, and there is a notion prevalent among English teachers today of the "native speaker of English" distinct from the rest of the world of English speakers. At the time the incidents caused me considerable distress, since I was lacking in confidence, aware of my accent, and I bore constantly in mind the fact that I was competing with teenagers who had no other responsibilities and who were fresh out of school. My writing, however, never reflected my lack of confidence.

The experimental novel *What Passing Bells* was completed while I did the English degree. The original draft was impressionistic, its form suggestive of a fractured society, of people in an apartheid system isolated from each other. It combined poetry with prose. Its purpose was to frustrate the reader's need for continuity, because this is precisely how we are frustrated in our understanding of the South African situation. I've seen other works published which are experimental and this reinforces my view that it isn't simply that publishers determine what is acceptable for some prescribed market, but they have a stereotype of how someone belonging to a specific group should write. One publisher's representative asserts very firmly that Black women write autobiographically. A Black woman experimenting with language and form has no business writing.

In the new Commonwealth, those writers who do not conform to these stereotypes are said to have been influenced by Western tradition, to have had an "English" as opposed to a "Bantu" or "Third World" education, or they are said not to be writing for the "people". These views are in current circulation among researchers and critics today. I've heard this said of Salman Rushdie, Dennis Brutus, Arthur Nortje, Chinua Achebe, etc. It is an evil. On the one hand it persuades us not to read certain writers; on the other it deprives us of sharing in our writers' achievements. But the crunch comes when we disregard Western tradition and publishers' stereotypes, and attempt to experiment — this isn't tolerated.

Two degrees and a teaching certificate made no difference to my prospects in the job market. I accepted work as a secretary for a large institution where I experienced racism and male dominance. It was inevitable that I should want to avoid these situations.

Nineteen eighty-four was my first year as a full-time writer. In that year I completely revised the "Bells" manuscript, wrote an article about prejudice in education, most of the essays on "Woman", and three short stories in a series "African in Exile". Each of the three stories is associated with a European work of art. I had in mind an African in exile wandering through the galleries in Europe and reminded of situations at home. "Poppy" is associated with *Field of Poppies*, "The Seed" with Van Gogh's *Old Woman in a Field* and "The Dove" with Picasso's *Child and Dove*.

Except for the one-off pieces that have appeared in *Kunapipi* [an arts periodical which places special emphasis on the new literatures written in English] I've had nothing published in England. When I submitted the "Bells" manuscript to a South African publisher, it was returned by the Customs.

A writer needs encouragement and a reading public. Encouragement for the writer is neither praise nor flattery; it can only come in the form of publication whether in newspapers, magazines, journals, or books. Nor does publication mean what it appears to mean to numerous presses and publishers: writing for nothing. Publication in newspapers, magazines and journals for a writer who expects to earn a living from writing means regular payment for short pieces of work while a longer work is in progress. How can a woman justify writing for nothing when she has children to support? Should a publisher or editor expect writers to contribute to a book without having budgeted for payment to the writers? Yet this is exactly how some publishers and editors do operate: in all the economic considerations for publication, the publisher, the printer, the stationer, the typesetter, the editor, receive remuneration, while the writer is not accounted for.

Why has it proved impossible for my work to be published in England? Is it a question of not being good enough? I like to think not. Many articles that appear in newspapers paraphrase what is published in scholarly journals. Women's magazines and the women's pages in newspapers feature articles that are without any depth and a great deal of mediocre fiction is published by some English literary magazines.

The treatment of new writers in England has resulted in an increasing number of writers coming together to assess, perform and publish their own work.

The situation of the Black woman writer in England has not gone unnoticed. I am now in contact with a group of Black women attempting to set up a publishing company with the purpose of correcting this imbalance. And the experience I've gained from dealing with racism and male dominance at work (and in schools) has resulted in the ethnic minority community inviting me to chair a group that promotes good relations between the races and equal opportunities for minority groups.

I have neither a room, a table, nor a corner of my home that I can call my own in which to write. After twelve years in the colonial atmosphere of York (York is to parochialism as art is to the Louvre, music to Vienna, philosophy to Greece), I have to decide whether it is better for me to return to South Africa and write within the confines of censorship but with the support of my family, or to remain in England.

At no stage in my life did I make a conscious decision to be a writer. Nor can I remember ever entertaining the notion or desire to be one. I write out of a deep sense of frustration.

Agnes Sam, 1985

from "WHAT PASSING BELLS"
The boy galloped.
Small, dark and wiry, he galloped.
On the pavement
To the corner
A wide arc
Down to his father
Back again.
Galloping furiously,
Elbows flapping
Tongue clucking
In the sunshine
To the corner
Down to his father
Back again.
Moving rhythmically.
His rhythm infectious.
The distance decreasing as his father neared the intersection.
They held hands and waited.

Once across he galloped ahead —

ya can't come with
ya can't come with

Then turned the corner.

The little girl disentangled her fingers.
Her expression anxious she glanced up at the man for approval
        before she dashed after the boy
Her hair and her short skirt billowing around her.
The man followed unhurriedly

Now with a hand clasped around each ankle of the boy straddling
        his shoulders.

                            We're going to the park, ja! ja!
                            We're going to the park, ja! ja!
                                    Ya can't come with
                                    Ya can't come with

The boy darted between the heavy brown gates that stood slightly
        ajar.
She hared after him.

The boy galloped
Looking back frequently
Laughing at her
On the narrow path crammed with little pebbles winding
        between the areas of grass.
She stumbled after him
Crying out
Unable to catch up with him
On the narrow path bordered by two rows of even-sized white-
        washed stones.

They crunched to a halt.

    Is it our turn?
She shouted above the noise of children playing
    Wait!
He sounded adult.

They stepped forward warily
Onto the grass
Lush and green
Neatly kept with a precise uniformity
And meticulously
Weeded
From the clumps of flowers growing tall and stately on its
    borders.

      Is it our turn?
She shrilled impatiently
Her attention fixed on brightly painted climbing frames
Shaped like space-ships and spiders
Swings, see-saws and slides alive with shrieking children.

Together they stepped
Wide-eyed
Up to the circle of short, stout poles that seemed to grow from the
      ground
And stood at the edging
Of thick, white rope that linked the poles to each other
Setting the play area apart from the park.

   Come on!
She urged crossly tugging insistently at his wrist.
   Wait!
He pulled back.
He was equally annoyed.
His eyes flashed from one end of the play area to the other.

A park attendant in navy-blue uniform walked by.
He wagged a playful finger at them.

They edged towards each other.
Her voice dropped to a disappointed whisper
   Isn't it our turn?
The boy put his finger to his lips:
   Sh!

As the attendant marched out of sight he sprang to life,
   Wowee! Look at 'em go!
   I'm tired!
She announced flatly and turned away
Her cheeks puffed out sulkily.
He grabbed her arm,
   He's gonna be sick! Looooooooooook! On the roundabout!

She shook herself free,
   I wanna go to Daddy,
   What did I tell ya?
He shrieked.
   Waah la! He's getting sick! What did I tell ya?
   I'm tired
She sighed.
Then she began kicking the pebbles onto the grass at his feet
Pouting her lips sullenly
With each movement she made.

   Then go back to Daddy
He retorted over his shoulder.
   This is great, just great. Hey! Hey! What's happening? Why all
      the screaming? Sissy!
He pointed sharply to a boy climbing backwards down the slide
   Look at the great big sissy! Waah la!
   Come with
She pleaded.
He ignored her.
His attention was elsewhere

Old men and women all dressed in white clustered onto the green
      grass on the other side of the pebbled path.

She placed herself squarely in front of him, moving her head with
      each movement of his, so that she continually blocked
   his view.
He sighed heavily
   Now what?
   Did you have a turn?
They turned simultaneously towards the smart tap
Of wood on wood
Her question forgotten as the old men and women commenced
      their game of bowls.

   Ooooh . . . look at 'em go. Swings are best, I tell ya. I love
      swings best of all.

Swings make me sick!
And saying this she quickly turned her back on the play area
Lifted her short skirt with a flourish
And pushed out her bottom with an emphatic —
    So there!

    I can go higher than that! Higher! Higher!
He challenged with his hands cupped around his mouth.

A man walked along the path, formed his grease-proof bag into a
        hard ball and aimed it at a "Keep-Your-City-Clean"
    litterbin.
    Did you go higher than that?
She asked him sweetly.
    Hey? Did you? Did you go higher than that?
He replied with a shriek.
    He's too scared to stand! Waah la!
Then he began clapping and chanting
    Too scared to stand!
    Too scared to stand!
    Too scared to stand!
    When'll't be our turn?
    Higher! Higher! Higher!
    When is it our turn?
    Stand and swing! Stand! Higher! Higher! I can go higher!
    How long must I wait then?
There was not much difference in their heights, but he cleverly
        slanted his head so that he appeared to be looking down
at her and said with exasperation in his voice,
    Dontcha know even?
He was shouting again
    I can go higher than that! Higher! Higher!
    How long did you wait then?
She leaned forward tilting her head
So that she could look into his face.
But when she saw that she had lost his attention once more
She angrily clapped her hands to her ears and screamed,
    Daddeeeee!

So that the children stopped playing to look at her.
  Agh, pipe down nonkie! When ya gonna grow up, hey?

The man walked up to them with the boy still straddling his
      shoulders.
She moved over to his side and put her hand trustingly in his.
The boy burst out excitedly,
  Gosh Dad! You sure missed something!
  How many times must I tell you?
He said, his voice evenly soft
  Dont — watch – them!

The children skipped away

                          We're going to the park
                          We're going to the park
                            Ya can't come with
                          Ya can't come with . . .
They raced on to the end of the park
Where it overlooked the lake
Where the two metal frames stood singularly alone
Dangling lengths of rusty chain
From which the wooden seats had been hacked when he had been
      a child.
                          Ya can't come with
                          Ya can't come with
                        'Cause you're afraid of the dark. Ja!
                                          Ja!

VALERIE BLOOM

Valerie Bloom was born in Clarendon, Jamaica, where she taught for three years before coming to England. She went to the University of Kent where she gained a first-class honours degree in English with African and Caribbean Studies.

Valerie's first book of poetry *Touch Mi; Tell Mi* was published by Bogle L'Ouverture in 1983 and since then she has had poems published in several anthologies. Her second book of adult poetry is due to be published in the near future. She has also written several children's poems and song lyrics for a musical based on the history of slavery and the cotton industry.

Over the last six years, Valerie has performed extensively throughout Britain. She has worked on radio in Jamaica and in England, including a regular feature on BBC Radio Manchester, and has appeared on television, both on ITV and on BBC2's "Ebony".

She is presently working as Multicultural Arts Officer with North West Arts, based in Manchester.

*   *   *

Almost every writer I have met has had the urge to write from childhood. Not many writers lived in the rural Jamaican town of Frankfield when I was a child, so for fear of being ridiculed I kept to myself the desire to create the same magic I had found in books from the minute I could read. I could and did give full rein to my imagination in my school compositions, but although we had to memorize and repeat parrot-fashion a poem a week, we were not encouraged to write our own. I therefore had no inclination to write poetry, even though I thoroughly enjoyed those I was asked to memorize, and even though I read many others for pleasure. My heart was set on becoming a novelist and/or short story writer.

Quite when I started performing Louise Bennett's dialect poetry in public, I cannot remember. Like many Jamaican schoolchildren, I had memorized many of these poems and can still recall the thrill of opening the newspaper one day to see my name in print after I had performed at a "Jamaica Nite" in the local primary school. My pleasure was only slightly diminished by the fact that the picture which accompanied the caption "Valerie Wright performing a dialect poem . . ." was not of me at all. It transpired that the photographer had run out of film before I went on stage. After that, until I left primary school, I was often asked to perform "Miss Lou's" poems at tea evenings, concerts and library committee meetings. I suppose that when I started writing poetry it was inevitable that I should be influenced by Louise Bennett.

Nobody was more surprised than I was when I wrote my first poem in 1978. Although I was determined to write, up till then my efforts had been confined to a few short stories, strictly for private perusal. My only attempts at poetry had been written in the style of Wordsworth and his contemporaries, whose works we had memorized at primary school. The peals of laughter from my sisters — who were my only readers then — convinced me that I should stick to prose. Then, one day in 1978 my family was swapping stories, as we often did. One, told by my mother, was particularly funny and I went to my room straight afterwards. Almost without being aware of what I was doing, I took pen and paper and began to write. In only a few minutes I had finished "Mek Ah Ketch Har" (see p.87). I was encouraged to enter it in the National Festival's Literary Competition and, thinking I had nothing to lose, I did. It won a bronze medal; by the next year it was being performed all around the island in the National Festival's Speech Competition and my poetry-writing career had begun.

The debt to Louise Bennett is obvious in that first poem, and indeed in most of the poems in my first volume. As in her work, most of the poems are humorous, but there is a strong element of social commentary in them as well. I deal both with individuals' vanity and hypocrisy and with wider issues relating to injustice in society (pp.91–3, "Yuh Hear 'Bout", "A Soh Dem Sey").

My more recent writing employs a wider range of techniques than the form regularly used by Miss Lou. The first time I departed from this model was in "Yuh Hear 'Bout", where a conversational style, extreme brevity and an apparently throw-away last line were necessary to create the bitter effect I wanted.

The next occasion I departed from what had been my normal style had a different but no less bitter source. I returned to Jamaica in 1983 for the first time in four years. Although the pleasure of seeing my family again was intense, the visit was marred by the murder of Michael Smith. I had known Michael in Jamaica, and we had performed together in London and Manchester. It seemed clear to me that Michael was a major international poet, but more particularly that he was taking Jamaican dialect poetry into new areas. I was stunned when I heard the news of his death on the radio, but the next day I sat down and wrote "For Michael". Like "Mek Ah Ketch Har", this poem took only a few minutes to write. There seemed no other way to start than with the title of the poem with which he was most associated, but which now took on a terrible new meaning. "Mi Cyan Believe It", and the rest of this tribute to him uses mainly his own lines rearranged, and has the style therefore of a Michael Smith poem.

Since then I have written in a number of different styles. Although "iambic quatrain with its ABCB rhyming scheme", which was the form I had taken from Louise Bennett and relied on in my early writing, carried with it a built-in sense of security borne of long familiarity, I feel more adventurous now. I feel sure I shall continue to use this form on occasion, but rather than automatically using it I now try to match the form I use for any particular poem with what I am trying to say in that poem. I have even had the confidence recently to attempt my first poem in Standard English, free from the fear that it would turn out as a sub-Wordsworthian Romantic pastiche. I am also writing a parallel poem in dialect dealing with the same subject matter. They look like being very different poems and I don't think that it would have been possible to write either poem in the other language form and retain its essential character.

Both of these poems are adult poems but were in a sense written for my young daughter. At the same time I have begun to write children's poems, and this has again led me to experiment with form, in particular with different rhythms.

The common factor in all of my poems is that they are written for performance rather than simply to be read on the page. This means that I have had to sacrifice some literary techniques to give the poems an immediacy which is easy to assimilate. It also means that only fifty per cent of the poems are actually on the page, the other fifty per cent being in the performance. Although this may make it difficult for anyone who has not seen a performance to appreciate fully the poems on the page if they cannot visualize the actions, it does not bar people who haven't seen a performance from appreciating the work. It could even be a good thing, as they are able to view it without preconceived ideas or interference and bring a fresh interpretation to the words. On the other hand, while I do not make compromises about the quality of the work, the performance element ensures that there is nothing obscure in the poems. This does not mean that the scope of a performance poet is limited, any more than is that of a dramatist.

I work within the old oral tradition that goes back to Africa, rather than the newer one of reggae and dub poetry. The differences are partly of rhythm: I usually use normal speech rhythms rather than the musical rhythms of dub music. The other difference relates to directness of approach. Dub poetry is poetry of protest which confronts issues of exploitation and injustice head-on. The work of dub poets such as Oku Onuora and Linton Kwesi Johnson has a rawness and a power which is very effective. However, I am happier with my own poems that rely on irony, such as "Yuh Hear 'Bout" and "A Soh Dem Sey", rather than those that use this direct approach.

In Jamaica the fact that my work was rooted in the oral tradition was no big news, for the tradition has endured unbroken, although customs (for example, families gathering round to tell stories on moonlit nights) are threatened by social change. In England the situation is very different. The old oral tradition seems to have been neglected or lost. My poetry appears to remind people of it. Especially when I perform to a "community audience" rather than a poetry-going audience. I often find that people, older people in particular, are astonishingly gratified. This is clearly not just a response to my work as such, but is because something has been restored which they felt had been left behind.

This suggests that poetry, or maybe just the use of authentic patois, touches deep nervesprings. It is clear that language is closely associated with identity. There has been a well-documented struggle in Jamaica (and the other Caribbean islands) to give status to the first language of the vast majority of the people. Apart from anything else, this has led to a close concern for the terminology related to language. Edward Kamau Brathwaite coined the term "Nation Language" to give dignity and status to the way we talk. Linguists use the technically correct "creole", though this is not a term used by ordinary people in Jamaica. Most Jamaicans refer to their first language as "patois", but I have never come across the term "patois poetry". "Dialect poetry" is a standard term, however, in Jamaica (Miss Lou's poems are sometimes referred to simply as "dialects"), and is the term I have used, though when referring to the language as a separate entity I have used "patois". I appreciate the reason why some people prefer other terms, but for me the struggle has been won. "Patois" and "dialect poetry" have a high value. There is no need to use a term to boost the status of the way we talk. It is a sign of greater self-confidence to be able to use the terms of the people without having to fear that these terms are in any sense disparaging.

Valerie Bloom
October 1985

MEK AH KETCH HAR

Onoo hole mi yaw, onoo hole mi good,
No mek mi get weh do,
For ah mus kill har if mi ketch har,
Dat mawga gal name Sue.

Onoo no tell mi fe shet mo mout,
Ah mus sleep a jail tenite!
Long time now she dah fool roun mi,
An teday ah gwine bus a fight.

Look how de gal come lable mi,
Look how she call me tief!
Jus' because she see mi a har kitchen
a tas'e har mah corn-beef.

An all a wi kno' har mah cyan cook,
so mi was jus' a try
see if mi coulda help dem out,
Mek sure de fat no dye.

For wi all memba las' Thursday nite
De hole o' dem nea'ly dead,
When dem done eat de tun corn-meal
Dem poison wid liquid lead.

Mi was jus' a try i' out,
Mek sure it was a'right,
Onoo let mi go mek a ketch har!
Dem gwine bury har before daylight.

Lawd! see har mah a come yah now!
Har pah a come wid har to!
Har brother, har sista an she herself,
A wha mi a go do?

Mercy! dem ha' one sobble-jack,
An one debbil ebba big crow-bar!
Mi done fah now, mi dead tenight,
A whey mi a go do Miss Flar?

Hide mi Miss Flar, hide mi,
No mek dem ketch mi please,
If dem ketch mi dem gwine kill mi
An yuh wi never be at ease.

A gawn dem gawn? Mi no see dem.
Dem 'fraid o' mi yuh kno'
Onoo let mi go mek a calla Sue!
Mek ah gi' har two big blow.

Ah gwine mek she kno' mi a big ooman,
A no yesterday mi bawn,
Lawd ha' massey, dem a come back,
Onoo gi mi pass, mi gawn!

Let Me Get Hold Of Her

Just hold on to me, hold me tight,
Don't let me get away, will you?
Because I'll kill her if I get hold of her,
That skinny girl called Sue.

Don't tell me to shut my mouth,
I'm sure to sleep in jail tonight!
For too long now she's been messing me around,
And today I'm going to have to fight.

Look at the way she's libelled me.
Look how she called me a thief!
Just because she saw me in her kitchen
Tasting her mother's corned beef.

And we all know her mum can't cook,
So I was just going to try
To see if I could help them out,
And make sure the fat wasn't dye.

For we all remember last Thursday night,
The lot of them were nearly dead,
When they'd eaten the turned-cornmeal*
They'd been poisoned with liquid lead.

I was just going to try it out,
To make sure it was alright,
Let go of me, let me get my hands on her,
They're going to bury her before daylight!

Lord, her mother's coming now,
Her dad's with her too!
Her brother, her sister and she herself,
What am I going to do?

Have mercy! They've got a sobble-jack†
And the devil of a big crow-bar!
I'm done for now, I'll be dead tonight,
What can I do, Miss Flar?

Hide me, Miss Flar, Hide me!
Don't let them catch me, please.
If they catch me they'll kill me,
Then you'll never feel at ease.

Have they gone? I can't see them.
They're afraid of me, you know.
Let me go, let me collar Sue,
Let me give her two big blows.

I'm going to let her know I'm a big woman,
It's not yesterday I was born,
Lord have mercy, they're coming back,
Out of my way, I've gone.

YUH HEAR 'BOUT?

Yuh hear bout di people dem arres
Fi bun dung di Asian people dem house?
Yuh hear bout di policeman dem lock up
Fi beat up di black bwoy widout a cause?
Yuh hear bout di MP dem sack because im
     refuse fi help
im coloured constituents in a dem fight
     'gainst deportation?
Yuh no hear bout dem?
Me neida.

---

* turned corn-meal — cornmeal cooked with salted cod and seasoning
† sobble-jack — whip made from the branch of the guava tree.

Did You Hear About?

Did you hear about the people they arrested
For burning down the Asian people's house?
Did you hear about the policeman they put in jail
For beating up the black boy without any cause?
Did you hear about the MP they sacked
because he refused to help
his black constituents in their fight
against deportation?
You didn't hear about them?
Me neither.

TRENCH TOWN SHOCK (A SOH DEM SEY)

Waia, Miss May, trouble dey yah,
Ban yuh belly, Missis, do.
Mi ha' one terrible piece o' news,
An mi sarry fe sey it consarn yuh.

Yuh know yuh secon' or t'ird cousin?
Yuh great-aunt Edith Fred?
Im pick up imse'f gawn a'pickcha show,
An police shoot im dead.

But a di bwoy own fault yah mah,
For im go out o' im way
Fi gawn fas' wid police-man,
At leas' a soh dem sey.

Dem sey im a creep oba di teata fence,
Dem halla "Who go deh?"
De bwoy dis chap one bad wud mah,
At leas' a soh dem sey.

De police sey 'tap or we opin fiah'.'
But yuh know ow di bwoy stay,
Im gallop back come attack dem,
At leas' a soh dem sey.

Still, nutten woulda come from i',
But wha yuh tink, Miss May?
Di bwoy no pull out lang knife mah!
At leas' a soh dem sey.

Dem try fi aim afta im foot
But im head get een di way,
Di bullit go 'traight through im brain,
At leas' a soh dem sey.

Dry yuh yeye, mah, mi know i hat,
But i happen ebery day,
Knife-man always attack armed police
At leas' a soh dem sey.

That's What They Say

O Lord, Miss May, trouble has hit us,
Bind your belly, ma'am, do.
I have some terrible news,
And I'm sorry to say it concerns you.

You know your second or third cousin,
Your great aunt Edith's Fred?
He took himself off to the cinema,
And the police shot him dead.

But it was the boy's own fault, you hear, ma'am,
For he went out of his way
To interfere with the police,
At least, that's what they say.

They saw him climbing over the fence,
They cried out, "Who goes there?"
The boy just let fly a swear word, ma'am,
At least, that's what they say.

The police said, "Stop or we'll open fire!"
But you know what boys are like today,
He rushed back and attacked them,
At least, that's what they say.

Still, nothing would have come out of it,
But what do you think, Miss May?
The boy pulled out a long knife, ma'am,
At least, that's what they say.

They tried to aim at his foot
But his head got in the way,
The bullet went straight through his brain,
At least, that's what they say.

Dry your eyes, ma'am, I know it hurts,
But it happens every day,
Knife-men always attack armed police,
At least, that's what they say.

FOR MICHAEL

Mi cyan believe it,
Mi sey mi cyan believe it
When yuh hear from di shout
One dead!
Who dead?
Mi nuh dead!
Yuh nuh dead!
So who dead?
Mikey dead!
An mi cyan believe it
But mi haffi believe it
For di newspaper cyah it
An di radio a shout it
An di people dem a wail it.
An mi ban mi belly an mi bawl
For di preacher man know it
An im noh fraid fi sey it
Ashes to ashes, dust to dust
An hey natty, natty,
Dem bury a piece a mi culture.

It's a hard road to travel
An a mighty long way to go
But yuh neva go nowhey
For yuh foot dis touch di road
An di whole a wi did see
Sey di road yuh did a walk
A di road whey wi fi tek
Back to wi roots and consciousness
But who coulda tell
Sey di stone eena di road
Coulda hab so much power
Fi tap yuh from walk
Fi tap yuh from talk.
Ten cent a bundle fi di callalloo dread, ten cent a bundle
But wi cyan eat callalloo whey fertilize wid blood
An wi cyan afford fi lose
No more prophet no more scribe
For ratta, ratta nuh bring back new life
An di pickney still a bawl
An di rent di deh fi pay
An when wi lose di prophet
Only Jesus know di way.

GRACE NICHOLS

Grace Nichols was born in 1950 in Guyana and is a short-story writer, journalist, novelist and poet. She has been living in Britain since 1977 and has had her poetry published in several anthologies and journals. She is the author of two children's books, *Trust You, Wriggly* and *Baby Fish and other Stories*. Her first novel, *Whole of a Morning Sky*, was published in 1986 by Virago, who also published her volume of poetry, *The Fat Black Woman's Poems* (1984). But her first and most celebrated volume remains *i is a long memoried woman*, for which she won the Commonwealth Poetry Prize in 1983.

*   *   *

Sacred Flame

Our women
the ones I left behind
always know the taste
of their own strength —
bitter at times it might
be

But I
armed only with my mother's smile
must be forever gathering
my life together like scattered beads.

What was your secret mother —
the one that made you a woman
and not just Akosua's wife

With your thighs you gave
a generation of beautiful children

With your mind you willed the crops
commanding a good harvest

With your hands and heart
plantain soup and love

But the sacred flame of your woman's
kra you gave to no man, mother
Perhaps that was the secret then —
the one that made you a woman
and not just Akosua's wife

      (i is a long memoried woman)

As a writer I feel strongly multi-cultural and very Caribbean. If I
have to describe myself as coming from a particular part of the
world, I like to think of myself as coming from the Caribbean.
Most of my work is created out of that culture which embraces so
much. The Caribbean has one of the richest, most fascinating
cultures you can hope to find anywhere; though this may sound
like a cliché, for me it's true. OK, it has its poverty and
backwardness, but just thinking about all the different cross-
influences and mixtures — Amerindian, African, Asian, European
— gets me high.

  I keep being amazed at how much of Africa still remains in the
Caribbean, when you consider the disruption caused by slavery
and the whole European colonizing experience. You have the
presence and influence of the indigenous people in the region too.
I feel a kinship with the Amerindian people of Guyana, for
example, their myths and legends. I've used some of their legends
in my children's stories. The Guyana hinterland is very much in
my psyche so that part of me feels a bit South American and the
incredible destruction of the Aztec/Inca civilization also informs
our heritage.

      . . . up past the Inca ruins

      and back again
      drifting onto Mexican plains

> the crumbling of golden gods
> and Aztec rites
> speak for themselves . . .

> ("Of Golden Gods")

Then of course you have the influences of the different immigrant groups who came out to the Caribbean: East Indians, Chinese, and Portuguese. So my voice as a writer has its source in that region. I feel a concern for the Caribbean and its economic and political future.

> Wake up Lord
> brush de sunflakes from yuh eye

> Back de sky and while Lord
> an hear dis mudda-woman cry
> on behalf of her presshah down people

> God de Mudda/God de Fadda/God de Sista
> God de Brudda/God de Holy Fire . . .

As a writer and poet I'm excited by language, of course. I care about language, and maybe that's another reason why I write and continue to write. It's the battle with language that I love. When it comes to writing poetry, it is the challenge of trying to create or chisel out a new language that I like. I like working in both standard English and creole. I tend to want to fuse the two tongues because I come from a background where the two worlds, creole and standard English, were constantly interacting, though creole was regarded, obviously as the inferior by the colonial powers when I was growing up, and still has a social stigma attached to it in the Caribbean.

I think this is one of the main reasons why so many Caribbean poets, including myself, are now reclaiming our language heritage and exploring it. It's an act of spiritual survival on our part, the need (whether conscious or unconscious) to preserve something that's important to us. It's a language that our foremothers and forefathers struggled to create and we're saying that it's a valid, vibrant language. We're no longer going to treat it with contempt or allow it to be misplaced.

I don't think the only reason I use creole in my poetry is to preserve it, however. I find using it genuinely exciting. Some creole expressions are so vivid and concise, and have no equivalent in English. And there comes a time when, after reading a lot of English poetry, no matter how fine (I love the work of quite a few English poets), I want something different; something that sounds and looks different to the eye on the page and to the ear. Difference, diversity and unpredictability make me tick.

I have a natural fear of anything that tries to close in on me, whether it's an ideology or it's a group of people who feel that we should all think alike because we're all women or because we're all black, and there's no room to accommodate anyone with a different view.

I can't subscribe to the "victim-mentality" either, which seems to like wallowing in "Look what they've done to us". It's true that black women have carried much more than their share of hardships along the way. But I reject the stereotype of the "long-suffering black woman" who is so strong that she can carry whatever is heaped upon her. There is a danger of reducing the black woman's condition to that of "sufferer", whether at the hands of white society or at the hands of black men. I know too many black women with a surmounting spirit and with their own particular quirkiness and sense of humour to know that this isn't true.

In the early days when I first started reading my poetry I was taken to task by a few women who wanted to know why I didn't write about or focus on "the realities" of black women in Britain: racial discrimination, bad housing, unemployment, etc., and this poem came as a kind of response to that:

OF COURSE WHEN THEY ASK FOR POEMS ABOUT THE 'REALITIES' OF BLACK WOMEN

> what they really want
> at times
> is a specimen
> whose heart is in the dust

a mother-of-sufferer
trampled/oppressed
they want a little black blood
undressed
and validation
for the abused stereotype
already in their heads

        or else they want
        a perfect song

I say I can write
no poem big enough
to hold the essence

        of a black woman
        or a white woman
        or a green woman

and there are black women
and black women

        like a contrasting sky

of rainbow spectrum

touch a black woman
you mistake for a rock
and feel her melting
down to fudge

cradle a soft black woman
and burn fingers as you trace
revolution
beneath her woolly hair

and yes we cut bush
to clear paths
for our children
and yes we throw sprat
to catch whale
and yes
if need be we'll trade

a piece-a-pussy
than see the pickney dem
in the grip-a-hungry-belly

still there ain't no
easy belly category

        for a black woman
        or a white woman
        or a green woman

and there are black women
strong and eloquent
and focussed

and there are black women
who always manage to end up
frail victim

and there are black women
considered so dangerous
in South Africa
they prison them away

        maybe this poem is to say
that I like to see
we black women
full-of-we-selves walking

        crushing out
        with each dancing step

the twisted self-negating
history
we've inherited

        crushing out
        with each dancing step

I'm also very interested in mythology. It has created certain images and archetypes that have come down to us over the ages, and I have observed how destructive, however inadvertently, many of them have been to the black psyche. As children we grew up with the all-powerful male white God and the biblical associations of white with light and goodness, black with darkness and evil. We feasted on that whole world of Greek myths, European fairy-tales and legends, princes and princesses, Snowhites and Rapunzels. I'm interested in the psychological effects of this on black people even up to today, and how it functions in the minds of white people themselves.

Once when I was taking part in a discussion on this subject, a white woman in the audience made the point that darkness was frightening. Children were afraid of the dark because they couldn't see in the dark. I agreed with her. I myself put on lights if I'm feeling a bit uneasy for some reason. But what the white imagination has done is to transfer this terror of darkness to a whole race. I'm fascinated, to say the least, how whenever a white person — whether writer, painter or dramatist — has to portray an evil, ugly or a monstrous character they inevitably make that character black. It's as if the white imagination can't help depicting this because that's the image that comes to mind in relation to evil or terror.

I think that white people have to be aware of this in their psyche and question it if they don't want to be trapped in this clichéd vision.

I feel we also have to come up with new myths and other images that please us.

Although *The Fat Black Woman's Poems* came out of a sheer sense of fun, of having a fat black woman doing exactly as she pleases, at the same time she brings into being a new image — one that questions the acceptance of the "thin" European model as the ideal figure of beauty. The Fat Black Woman is a universal type of figure, slipping from one situation to the other, taking a satirical, tongue-in-cheek look at the world:

> Shopping in London winter
> is a real drag for the fat black woman
> going from store to store
> in search of accommodating clothes
> and de weather so cold

> Look at de frozen thin mannequins
> fixing her with grin
> and de pretty face salesgals
> exchanging slimming glances
> thinking she don't notice
> ("The Fat Black Woman Goes Shopping")

Literature isn't a static thing. The myths of old were created by the poets of old and remain powerful sources of imagination, to be drawn on again and again. Odysseus in his rolling ship did a lot for mine as a child and I am grateful. But we have to keep on creating and reshaping. We have to offer our children something more than gazing at *Superman 1*, *Superman 2*, *Superman 3* and possibly *Superman 4*, so that when they look out on the world they can also see brown and black necks arching towards the sun. So that they could see themselves represented in the miraculous, and come to sing their being.

In *i is a long memoried woman*, the woman is something of a mythic figure. She breaks the slave stereotype of the dumb victim of circumstance. She is a woman of complex moods who articulates her situation with vision. Her spirit goes off wandering, meeting women from other cultures. She's a priestess figure and employs sorcery when necessary.

> I require an omen, a signal
> I kyan not work this craft
> on my own strength
> alligator teeth
> and feathers
> old root and powders
> I kyan not work this craft
> this magic black
> on my own strength
> Dahomney lurking in my shadows
> Yoruba lurking in my shadows
> Ashanti lurking in my shadows
> I am confused
> I lust for guidance
>
> ("Omen")

At this point I must say that it isn't easy writing about myself as a writer and the piece very nearly "not got done". Immediately after I was asked by Lauretta, I began to suffer from what is conveniently known as "writers' block", even though I was at first very enthusiastic about the idea. The truth is, I don't like answering too many questions about my work and how I work. Half of the time I really don't know the answers. In any case I believe that my feelings on a range of issues come out much better in my poems and writings. Poetry, thankfully, is a radical synthesizing force. The erotic isn't separated from the political or spiritual, and a lot gets said.

It's difficult to answer the question "Why I write" because writing isn't a logical activity. It's a compulsion like a disease that keeps you alive. At a simple conscious level I would say that I write because writing is my way of participating in the world and in the struggle for keeping the human spirit alive, including my own. It's a way of sharing a vision that is hopefully life-giving in the final analysis.

In writing, I feel that I have some control over the world, however erroneous this might be. I don't have to accept things as they are, but can recreate the world a little more to my own liking. I don't have to accept a world that says that the black woman is invisible, for example, or a world that tries to deny not only black women but women on the whole, the right to participate in the decision-making necessary for change and an improved quality of life. I can introduce my own values. I can write against stereotypes as I've done with *The Fat Black Woman's Poems*.

Questions such as "How do you see yourself? Do you see yourself as Black first or as a Woman first?" sometimes asked by other women freeze up the brain and become irritating because it seems like arbitrary cross-examination. It isn't something you even sit down and think about — "Now am I black first or am I woman first?" These make up one's essential being, whatever that might be. "Am I a committed writer?" I think I am committed to my own truth. "Which is more important to me, the women's struggle or the fight against neo-colonialism and political repression?" I can't compartmentalize myself. I hate all forms of oppression. South Africa makes me feel chronically ill inside. I can't shut it out. And if a woman is being oppressed, say by her man at home, then that personal immediate oppression is just as hateful as the one by the state.

"Do I write as a 'woman' or simply as a 'writer'?" I don't really know but I believe that my perceptions cannot help but be influenced by my sex, race, cultural background and a heap of other factors, like the kind of childhood I had. Life is a mystery to me too. I myself am still working towards clarification. Maybe if I had all the answers I wouldn't be writing at all.

I IS A LONG-MEMORIED WOMAN REVIEWED BY PETER FRASER

It is a pleasure to review and recommend this poetry book by a West Indian writer, now living in England. Grace Nichols covers much the same ground as Edward K. Brathwaite's *The Arrivants* but focuses on those rather shadowy figures who appear in that work, women. It is an odyssey from Africa to the Caribbean during the period of slavery.

Grace Nichols's work is a long poem of great ambition. It takes us from Africa to the Haitian Revolution, ending with the recognition:

> I have crossed an ocean
> I have lost my tongue
> from the root of the old
> one
> a new one has sprung.

Africa is a memory of what has been lost, both of the good customs and practices and of the men "the colour of my own skin" who stole and traded other African men and women: "No it isn't easy to forget what we refuse to remember/Daily I rinse the taint of treachery from my mouth." Africa is also the place whose "old ones/turn against me in my dreams". The poet's attitude to

Africa is therefore not the simple rejection or acceptance of everything African that tend too often to dominate discussions. The experience of African women during slavery is linked to the earlier oppressions of the original American and Caribbean populations and specifically to those of Guyanese Indians. The acceptance that oppression came from men in general as well as slave-holders leads to a much more subversive view of the world than most men can achieve: "Yet even now/ the Gods of my people/grow cold, turning/with anger/I have not forgotten/them/I have not forsaken/them/But I must be true/to the dark sign/of my woman's nature/to the wildness of my/solitude and exile."

Complex too is the treatment of the means to end oppression. For these purposes Africa becomes a resource; the cunning of Anansi and the knowledge of sorcery and poisons are deployed to defeat the slave holders. But the consequences of violence are not celebrated: "Under the scarlet blossoms/of the poincianas/there are bodies . . ./quite headless/I cross myself/I sprinkle waters of purification/I close the eyes of the children with my lips/I lead them quickly away." Despite injustice and the harm inflicted on her, the vision of the future remains a humane one: "It isn't privilege or pity/that I seek/It isn't reverence or safety/quick happiness or purity/but/the power to be what I am/a woman/charting my own futures/a woman/holding my beads in my hand."

I look forward to more work from this splendid poet.

MARSHA PRESCOD

Marsha is a young Black woman who came to England as a small child with her parents during the wave of migration from the Caribbean by Black pioneers during the 1950s. She lives and works in London. She tries in her writing to analyse our situation, as Africans in the Diaspora, and her aim is to play whatever part she can in improving that situation, and to encourage others to do so too. To this end, many of her poems have a deadly serious message wrapped in a humorous package. The humour and the straightforward style are an attempt both to reflect the ways of talking of the community in which she grew up, and to make the ideas that stimulate her writing accessible and easy to absorb. She feels that writing and reading — like talking and listening — should not have a special mystique attached to them, and that artists are an integral part of their community and society. "Art is not, in our culture, something removed from everyday life. It's not highbrow, or obscure, or only for an elite. That's why despite being amongst the poorest people on this earth, we've had such a massive influence on the culture of other people, even those who oppress us. Black people are very creative, and our creativity is dynamic, beautiful, and down to earth."

*   *   *

Writing about writing seems a bit artificial. Being asked how I see myself as a writer, and why I write, seems like being asked how I see myself as a talker, and how I talk. Writing for me is like talking, first to myself, then to other people. I want to talk to Black people here, and in Africa, America and the Caribbean, for starters. Then I want to talk to the Black people who've lived in certain parts of the world for centuries that I didn't know about when I was growing up, like those settled in parts of South-East

Asia, in Russia, in the southern parts of India, in remote bits of China. I see my writing in that way. As I can't physically talk to lots of different people in different places at once, and as I can't afford to run up *that* kind of phone bill, I'm writing. So when you ask me how I see myself as a writer, I'd have to say as someone trying to get certain thoughts across to our people wherever they're scattered. And then, of course, there's what I want to talk about.

What I want to talk about isn't new or startling, it's what we're preoccupied with a lot of the time: who we are, what is happening to us, what has happened to us, and what can we do about it. What mistakes we're making. Any time Black people gather to socialize, if it's a scene that allows for people to sit down and chat, these topics come up, arguments occur, everyone's got their own ideas about what we should do. We're very reflective people, and I suppose that's hardly surprising. After all, if you're in a jam, unless you're an idiot you wonder how you got into it and how to get out. And we've been in a jam for a hell of a long time. I want to add my bit to the discussion we're always having. But then, I was always like that: whenever there was a party, and people would be gathered in the kitchen, away from the dancers, arguing about the world and what was wrong with it, pretty soon I'd be in there, piping up. Even when I was small, and it was big people talking (and you know about how big people feel about children butting into their conversations!) I was always joining in and listening in to big women's conversations. When my mother went to the hairdresser's, she would take me along. While everybody would be sitting around, having their hair washed, and greased, and the hot combs heated up, there would be really, really interesting conversations about life, children, men, work. I would be in a corner, supposedly reading a comic or book, but drinking it all in.

As for what might be called moral compulsions involved when I write, the moral compulsions are to try not to let myself down or to let Black people down by writing anything that is sensational in a scandalous way, or distorts or damages our experience. You know, not to be involved in what I call the movement to encourage a kind of neo-colonialism in literature. This is the situation where, instead of white people writing racist stuff about us, you get a subtler thing with people who are not white, and who have come out of a colonial experience, peddling the same rubbish under the guise of serious political analysis. This sort of writing tells those who oppress us what they most want to hear, that in some way the oppression is justified, and they can keep on doing what they're doing.

If asked what major influences have made a serious impact on my creativity, my answer is: Living. I mean that seriously. It would be very difficult to point to just a few influences, there are so many. Some of them happened before I was even born; they've shaped me because they've shaped us as a people. Some influences are the ones you'd expect — family, friends, the surroundings I grew up in. How I grew up, and how I *didn't* grow up. I'm still finding new influences all the time.

My only experience of life so far is being a Black woman. That shapes my writing, and that's good. I don't understand the people who have to run away from these sort of things, and talk crap like "I don't just want to be a Black writer," or they don't want to be viewed as a woman writing. What they're really saying is that they're worried that if they write from a Black woman or man's perspective, it won't seem universal. When you write from our perspective you are writing as a person, and our past and our present takes in things that everyone can relate to — tragedy, hope, despair, suffering, joy, you name it.

It may seem that I'm suggesting that Black writers or women writers must write from a particular perspective. But not really. I'm saying that when we write, we'll find certain experiences shaping our writing whether we like it or not. The intelligent thing is to understand that and work with it, not try to deny it. People preoccupied with being seen as "just writers" dealing with the "universal" are really using code, and sometimes they don't even realize that. It's a way of saying they're worried that if they write about matters specific to African people, white folks won't read it, and therefore it won't be literature; if they write about women's lives and feelings, white men won't relate to it, and it won't be art. If you're talking, however, about healthy development as an individual or as a people, then you can't afford to have those sort of preoccupations because they mean that you're viewing yourself through other people's eyes and that if you can't see yourself reflected in their eyes, then you don't exist.

At times I've been asked if I feel most besieged as a woman or as a Black. Some of the greatest tests of my skill in survival have come from living in a white racist country. No doubt about it. After all, my great-great-grandmother wasn't hauled on to a boat because the slavers were sexist, otherwise the Black women would have been taken and the Black men would have been left. In the Caribbean, America and South America, "sex equality" prevailed in so far as we too got a chance to work in the fields and on the plantations, to feel the whip, and to plan raids and escapes, just like the men. The extra burden of sexism of course meant that as well as all that, both during slavery and after, we also had the burden of domestic work. And, as one woman I recently talked to from a group interested in publishing women's writing in New York remarked to me, 'As far as our right to have children as and when we wanted was concerned, the master felt that our wombs belonged to them — so we'd end up having two sets of children, ours and 'theirs'.''

The pattern wasn't that much different for Black women after slavery either. Sometimes, older Black women living here talk about how women they knew had to work in the kitchens and laundries of the people running the colonies, and how a little sex was something the bosses felt they had a right to. You either did it, so your children could get fed, or else . . . You read about these things (though they're usually half-buried) when you read novels, or other literature about Black women working in a domestic setting for Whites in America (especially, but not exclusively, in the deep South) and in South Africa and in parts of the African continent which were subjected first to colonialism and later to neo-colonialism. This kind of thing was, and in some countries still is, common. Since our contact with the West began to take place to any significant extent, we've always caught hell as Black people, and then a little extra hell as women. If I'd been born a Black man anywhere in the western hemisphere, I'd have caught hell. So when I feel "besieged" (which isn't the term I'd use to describe it), it's mostly due to racism. That being said, the extra agony Black women experience inside and outside our community, stemming from the male compulsion to dominate women, is something that we'll have to deal with if we want to be strong, and free ourselves and progress. We'll have to deal with it before it deals with us.

In my writing, I try to show the danger of the situation we're in as Black people so that those who hear or read it will address themselves to that issue. So in "Death by Self-Neglect" (my favourite poem) I show how Black men and women are being brutalized, imprisoned and murdered all around the world . . . with the blame then being put on us for our misfortune. I also want them to address themselves to the issue of how Black women are being treated too and in "Love Story — Part Two" I poke fun at a particular type of behaviour some men in our community indulge in, the men who like to collect women in numbers to exploit them emotionally and sexually. I try to show how women can put their heads together and work out a way to really *deal* with them.

There is talk about a new explosion of Black British writing but there isn't a new explosion at all. If I can bump into a Black woman writing poetry at seventy-six years of age, and if I can read in some of the more progressive history books that we've been in Britain on and off for centuries, then it's quite likely that Black people in Britain have been writing for as long as we've been here. Whether the writing has always been published, of course, is another matter. As we're not in control of the publishing scene, the appearance of our work is subject to fashion, and whether we are in fashion or not. So I don't believe there's any new explosion, as such, just that the door has opened a little, little bit. I don't regard myself as "Black British" but rather as African, a person of African descent, living in Britain.

Then there is the question of standards. We have our own standards of excellence. I don't know whether they are the same as standards for other people's writings. Probably not, because a lot of people who are not Black don't know how to handle our stuff. They have no idea about our community; they won't do market research or read books from Africa, America or the Caribbean on Black Literary Criticism. They think liberal thoughts are enough and put out our work any old way, without proper editing. This means that work gets published that should not be published. (I hope this anthology is not going to be like that. I expect to see some rigorous editing, and I expect you to keep this bit in too!)

As a part-time writer, I have no neatly arranged schedule with a clear-cut routine. I have to fit in writing amongst the other aspects of living: my job, domestic life and a social life. And I'm basically a lazy writer, which adds to the problem. I write in short, concentrated bursts, and then do nothing for ages. I write a lot when travelling from one place to another, on buses or trains. I'm in a hurry with the writing, because I don't know how long I'll be alive, so I can't take it for granted that I'll always have plenty of time. The reality of our existence as a people is that you start to feel pressure from an early age. And you don't get a lot of time. To people who want to write I would say: think of the odd minutes you may have during your waking hours and use them to write. To scribble down ideas, to make notes, to do drafts, anything. If you've got a good family or friend, show them things you've done. If you don't like that idea, look for a writers' workshop, like the one I went to in Brixton at Black Ink, and join that. Other writers will be eager to help you once it's clear that you will help them assess their work, and they will criticize your work constructively rather than destructively. Decide whether you are writing just for yourself or for other people as well. Decide whether what you do is writing that is meant to be read, or writing that is meant to be said. If you're worried about putting it directly on to the page, you can talk into a tape recorder, as if you were having a conversation, and play it back and write it down — a very famous writer, Richard Wright, used to do that. Don't fret about your spelling; you can go over it with a good dictionary afterwards. Don't worry that you're too old, too young, or things like that. The youngest writer I met was eight, the oldest in her seventies. If you've got a story to tell, tell it.

A writer has responsibilities to the people she/he writes about, as well as to the readers. Black writers have the responsibility to be accurate when they tell our story. They can use any form — poetry, prose, autobiography, fiction. But they mustn't distort it. I don't like people who paint a picture by only dwelling on the corners of it. There must be a complete picture. I don't want to read men writing as if the attack on their manhood by this society is *the* problem. That's what I mean by dwelling on the corner of a picture, and not giving us the whole picture. And also, of course, there's the responsibility of not telling people to do things in your writing that you wouldn't do yourself. That's a very easy thing to do, to let your pen run away with you, and tell people to burn their boat whilst you're sailing in yours. So I try to think about things like that, because writing can lead to action. Above all, I try not to write things I don't feel.

EXILES

Forty years in the factory.
Thirty years on the bus,
Twenty years with machinery,
They don't make them any more like us.

Happy to know which place to go,
Canada, US and Britain,
Whether is canal to build,
War to fight,
Land to till,
We eager to make we heaven.

Small fish in an ocean
Of greed, and gold,
All we dreaming is how to get rank.
So, is families wasted,
An health all gone,
Whilst we putting we lives in the bank.

An when you hear the shout —
We can't get out,
Our pride and spirit get break.
At home prices too high,
An no jobs left to try,
Here,
We is crippled by the Welfare State.

Is a little beer here,
Little dominoes there,
And a lot of funeral to follow.
Having ketch as ketch arse,
Just a pensioners pass,
An a old folks home come tomorrow.

Forty years in the factory,
Thirty years on the bus,
Twenty years with machinery,
Yes . . .
They don't make them any more like us.

WOMANIST BLUES: (For those
feminists who would ignore race and
class)

Let's get together, Sister,
March with heads and shoulders high,
Let's get together, Sister
As my crops and children die.

We're in the same movement,
Moving, moving for our gain.
Suffering oppression, honey
But yours and mine just ain't the same.

Let's get together, Sister,
Explore your sexuality.
Let's get together, Sister,
While you define my sex for me.

We're gonna grab the Power,
You from your man, me from mine.
You'll get the wealth, technology,
Whilst I'll get a damn hard time.

Let's get together, Sister,
As you treat me and mine like dirt.
Let's get together, Sister,
Now Capital has donned a skirt.

Let's get together,
Let's get together,
Let's get together,
SISTER!

UNTITLED

I dont want to get into
the tyranny,
(the tyranny)

Of phone call waiting,
trying,
Not to show the caring.

. . . do not want to get into
the tyranny,
(the tyranny)

Of meeting for 'dates',
and trying hard
to be the one who's late.

. . . not want to get into
the tyranny
(the tyranny)

Of am-I-chasing-him
or-is-he-chasing-me
and-which-of-us-will
win?

. . . . . . want to get into
the tyranny
(the tyranny)

Of red hot possession
and 'I'll tell you *everything*
about my life' type confession.

. . . . to get into
the tyranny
(the tyranny)

Of rows and cries,
and blows,
the accusations
and the lies.

. . . . get into
the tyranny
(the tyranny)

Of sullen stares,
long silences,
Regrets of secrets shared.

. . . . into
the tyranny
(the tyranny)

Of 'I love you,
and are you *really*
sure my darling
that you love me too?'

No.

Don't want to get into
the tyranny,
the tyranny,
(the tyranny)
(the tyranny)

Death by Self Neglect

Wus a group a bigshot whitemen talking,
From de US an Europe an so,
Dey was all lookin terribly trubble,
As if dawg eat dey mudder-you know.

Well, de gen'ral from Uraguay stan up,
An he gaze plenty hard at de rest.
"Look, we ha' to sort out all dese darkies,
Cos dey puttin we patience to test."

"Boy, yu talkin' too true!" cry de Adm'ral,
"I for one here ain frighten to say,
Dese damn niggers so evil an wicked de world round,
Dey deading to spite we today!"

Ev'ry man dere head nod in agreement,
Dey was cultured, knew where dey stood,
An in all of dere various countries,
A conspiracy treaten de good.

De American sheriff look vex-vex,
"Boy, I know what yu mean!" he reply,
"Dey does fling demself straight on we gunbut!
Dey does poke out dey own blasted eye!"

"Yes, some blacks so incredibly spiteful,
Dey does shoot dey own self in de head,
An does purposely fall out of windows,"
De Sout' African minister said.

Den de man from great britan did rise up,
An a silence fall, "braps!" on de crowd.
When he speak, he whole body did tremble,
An his voice was too low to call loud.

"Allyu tink yu have problem?" he murmur,
"But yu ain have no real cause for strife,
Now de breed a blax we have in englan,
Put we all dere in fear a we life!"

"We does give dem de best of we housing,
Wid fresh air tru de roofing an thus,
An dey gettin de choicest of jobs too,
In de sewers an sweatshops an bus."

"Do you tink dem damn rascals is grateful?
Not a bit of it!" he shake his head.
"When dey force us to fling dem in prisn,
Dey dehydrate till we find dem dead!"

All de bigshots were nat'rally upset,
"Why dese darkies so wicked?" dey cry.
"We've tried so much good kindness for four hundred years,
An dey still go an selfishly die."

De millions of black dead don't answer,
Well, dey can't, tru dere shackles an chains,
But dey chil'ren an gran'chilren busy,
Wid dey skills an dey guns . . . an dey brains.

(*Land of Rope and Tory*, Akira Press, 1985)

MAY THE FORCE BE WITH YOU

If allyu want to keep yu carnival,
Wid yu jump-up, yu fete, yu roti,
An a chance to meet up wid yu macumere an ting,
All yu key spar who yu ain see for years,
Yu mus remember.

Any gatherin of Black people in dis town,
dus make dem nervous.
De only Blacks who ain criminals,
is entertainers, sportsmen, or Police.

So.

Nex' year, we go bring out a band.
We goin to have a maas to end all maas.
Two hundred tousand Black

man, woman an child, dress in dark blue.
Yes, de maas we playing is "Police", and
de theme of de band is, "Law and Order".

So when dey turn on de telly,
To see how many people riot for carnival,
All dey go see is two hundred tousand *Police*,
going dung de road.
Singing, drinking rum, whining, dancing.
Dey ain go be able to tell,
Who is de real police, an who is de maas police.

De Press gon go mad,
(Because you know dey like to take de same fucking
picture every year of Police at carnival)
De Commissioner, de Home Sec'etry, an de Prime Minister
Gon declare how community policing is a BIG success.
An dey go be right, because, for dat day,
De whole community go turn policeman.

An we Black people, go get to keep we carnival.

(*Apples and Snakes*, Pluto Press, 1984)

LAND OF ROPE AND TORY REVIEWED BY DOROTHEA SMARTT

Marsha Prescod has been living and working in England since the
1950s. She was encouraged initially by the Black Writers'
Workshop in Brixton and has been writing poetry since 1980.
Brent Black Music Workshop helped her to develop her own style
and confidence as a "performance poet". *Land of Rope and Tory*
is a collection of several years' work she has performed around the
country. She writes first for Blackpeople, using our humour to
win over those of us whose only (alienating) experience of poetry
was perhaps at school.
She covers a range of experience and politics in her work,

commenting on the lives and concerns of Blackpeople in struggle. All of her work is powerful and thought-provoking, it catches up with your thoughts and it left me nodding my head in recognition. Among the poems that moved me particularly is "Death by Self-Neglect", which is Marsha's favourite — and her personal preference for the title of this collection. She describes this as the "second and best poem I ever wrote". The title is taken from the coroner's verdict of the death of Richard "Cartoon" Campbell while in police custody. Through her poem she draws out some of the universality of our experience, letting " . . . a group of bigshot whitemen talking . . ." from Uraguay, America, "Sout' Africa" and "great britain' do the rest.

In "Warrior Woman's Song" I felt she touched on the economic, sexual and cultural abuse of our peoples and our land, reminding us of what can be and is Blackwomen's unique contribution to the survival of our peoples. "They're Playing Our Song" reminds us of the "slavery" of capitalism and how it is reflected in our lives today. I liked "Old Timers" for not letting us relegate our elders to a "dead" past, reminding us of their struggles — uprisings and "riots" didn't happen only now, within our generation "in Brixton"! "Love Story" (Parts One and Two) carries on our womanist traditions of commenting, to good effect, on our relationships and experiences with Blackmen.

I liked all of Marsha's work, my enjoyment reinforced by having also seen her in performance in the past. Blackwomen have "herstorically" used humour, as a tool of survival, to deal with horrors of our loss, and to pass on our skills and strategies. Marsha's work is about us recognizing the racism around us, and the need to tell and re-define our experiences in our own words, which she sums up in this "untitled" piece:

UNTITLED

For us to be free
we have to know we
don't let anyone "ethnicize" us,
into them marginal categories.

Our positive self cannot be,
through negative definition,
saying, "Well, we're not them"
to work out own position.

Don't look to *his*-tory,
to discover our existence.
Don't hide in another's ideasology,
to develop our own resistance.

For us to be free,
we have to know we.
Our own truth
our own strength,
And our

black,
black,
black,
black

creativity!

If you feel urged to action, perhaps you'll take Marsha's advice
and go out and order our books for libraries and "institutional-
ize" our presence" so that in twenty years' time we'll not be
invisible to our children, as the Black communities of twenty to
thirty years ago appear to be to us. We can also give our children
some of the humour that is and has been a strong part of our
survival.

THE COLLECTIVE: BEVERLEY BRYAN, STELLA DADZIE AND SUZANNE SCAFE

Beverley Bryan was born in Jamaica in 1949 and came to England when she was ten. For fifteen years, she has taught in primary and further education. At present, she is teaching adults in south London. Beverley was a founder-member of the Brixton Black Women's Group and has been active in Black, community and women's politics since the late 1960s. She has two sons and lives in south London.

Stella Dadzie was born in 1952. She has an English mother and a Ghanaian father. For six years, she worked in a London comprehensive, teaching Modern Languages. She also taught at a centre for young offenders for two years. Stella currently teaches Black Studies and co-ordinating courses for the unemployed and for Black women at a north London college. She has an MA in Afro-Caribbean history/African literature. She is a founder member of OWAAD (Organization of Women of Asian and African Descent). She lives in north London and has a son.

Born in Jamaica in 1954, Suzanne Scafe has taught English in both Jamaican and English secondary schools. She now teaches at a college in south London. Suzanne has been a member of the Brixton Black Women's Group for several years and has worked with the Committee of Women for Progress in Jamaica. She lives in south London.

*   *   *

WRITING AS A COLLECTIVE

When we were originally approached to contribute to this book and to consider our experience as writers, our initial amusement at the idea of the three of us having anything to say about our work gave way to some misgivings as to the reasoning behind such an exercise. Who would contribute to such a book? How much was this an imitation of the Black American experience? What would we possibly have to say about writing? These questions did not come from a desire to denigrate the growing achievements of Black women writers but we definitely wanted to be sure that the phenomenon we were being asked to comment on had some substance and was not just a passing media fancy. In any case we were reassured that we were being too modest as people who had just written "a best seller". After a few weeks of intermittent reflection, we came to a decision that perhaps we did have something to say about the writing process — something that was unique to our experience of collective writing, that might be useful to understanding the form, style and structure of our book.

In describing our own experiences, we have to first knock on the head some of the assumptions that have been made in reviews and interviews. Many seem to assume that we had approached the task of writing as three individuals whose main ambition was to make a name for ourselves; that we were now experts in the field and must therefore have something definitive to say about "the Black woman's experience"; and that we were now fully committed to a career as writers, and must be busy dashing off the next book. None of these things apply so simply and directly to us, but what these assumptions seem to suggest is a complete failure to understand what racism and sexism actually mean in practice for Black women who write — how it affects what, how, and even how much we put on paper. The kind of subject matter we want to tackle might now be more acceptable, but has not always been palatable to any part of the white media; the kind of voices we speak through will not compromise for a readership that might include white people; the very limited time we have available after the day's work and family chores will not enable us to write. On a personal and individual level, a part of the difficulty is about finding the time and space to cram a few coherent lines into *any* part of the day and night. Another part of the obstacle is about how we allow ourselves to become so intimidated by those paralysing assumptions that we don't consider ourselves able to take on such a task and complete it to any satisfactory degree. A disregard for these real problems and contradictions will only serve to perpetuate all those notions which mystify the writing process and further keep us silent and invisible. If we do anything, we must show the slow, painful, sometimes tedious and occasionally illuminating path we took to produce *The Heart of the Race*. In doing so we have to look critically at ideas about the role of the writer, the notions of writers as an exclusive breed and even their accepted status as expert.

First, if we consider the role of the writer, we have to say that none of us grew up with any conscious desire to become writers in print. The task seemed too daunting and time was too precious to spend on such an ephemeral activity. That was not to say we had not all written something we thought very precious in the privacy of our own rooms, but the urge "to go public" was not something we could or even wanted to sustain. We had also all written anonymously for many years for our own journals such as *Speak Out* and *Fowaad* but this was seen as part of a political commitment rather than an exercise in self-expression. Perhaps we just didn't take ourselves seriously enough! How then did we persuade ourselves to embark on such a mammoth task?

When Virago commissioned us in 1980, it was at a time which was really a highpoint of activity in terms of the organizing that Black women were doing. OWAAD had just been successfully launched, new women's groups were being set up and a lot of women were speaking up in these organizations. As individuals, the three of us were deeply involved in this work. Suzanne not yet in the group had recently returned from Jamaica and was trying to re-orientate herself to life in Britain, to find work and a place to live; Beverley had a new-born baby, a new course of study and was working with a group to set up the first Black women's centre; Stella, after some exhausting work with OWAAD and on education campaigns, was suffering the first stages of morning sickness. Our lives were full and we had enough to keep us active and occupied. Why did we agree to do it? It was precisely because we were active in our communities that the book became an important task to accomplish. Black women, as a group and as individuals, have made significant gains which we felt had been undervalued and had largely gone unrecognized. Because we had no media to rely on, what we now saw were these victories passing into folk memory as sisters died, moved, or left the country. The idea of a book that would underscore our powerful presence here was greeted with great enthusiasm. What we wanted to do was to set down those gains and give the respect and dignity that was due to sisters past and present who had made all our struggles possible.

From the beginning, the book was seen as a collective effort. The nature of the project determined the mode of writing. We took it on as we had taken on a whole range of other tasks and campaigns — a project that would involve pooling, sharing and articulating our ideas and experiences. This was how we had always written. We did not expect to see our own individual style or our favourite words emerging as dominant. We would write and give our writing up for criticism, for illustration and development. The end product would therefore represent all that we as a group wanted to say, all that came out of our discussions. That was why we initially intended to have none of our individual names on the printed book. In fact, the three of us who originally signed the contract — Beverley, Stella and Gerlin [Bean] — saw ourselves as merely representing a body of Black women who would ultimately be involved in the work. We would be living and shaping the book as we went through. With this way of writing accepted, and as it was to be about the *lives* of Black women, interviews were to be an integral part of the book's form and structure. They were to add a whole chorus of voices that would underscore the statements being made. Even from this early stage we saw the interviews as forming an integral part of the text, a part that would not be read as separate. We wanted to interweave analysis and experience, to show not only how we struggled through but why it was possible.

"The Book Collective" thus began with six or so members. There were continual calls for help and many sisters did express interest, but again there were so many different pulls on our time and energy that it was difficult to sustain such a large commitment. Perhaps the idea of being in print hardly seemed real.

Virago itself had been in existence for just five years as the only women's publishing house. The idea of women writing was still new and, with our experience of British society, the idea of Black women writing was even more remote. Even the writers we accept now as established, such as Toni Morrison, Buchi Emecheta, Alice Walker or Toni Cade Bambara, were not part of the political or literary consciousness of the time. We had no real models or guides. It was therefore not surprising that we allowed ourselves to be intimidated by public writing. Added to this, collective writing is not always the easiest of options. The mechanics of the process mean that sometimes a chapter has to be divided at the planning stage and each section written by an individual before being discussed, put together and discussed again. At other times the chapter has to be drafted by one person, written by another and rewritten yet again by another. In this way ideas are discussed and researched, examined and re-explained, until often they are thrown out. Couple this with the pressure of knowing that you are producing the first public record of Black women's lives in Britain and it will be clear how overwhelming the task seemed. This pressure, in the beginning, affected the style and tone of the initial work on the book.

We began with a large historical introduction to put the interviews that were to follow in their proper context. We spent months on this first chapter, trying to find the right approach, the right interpretation of the information and the right wording. We distanced ourselves from writing and worried about our sources and footnotes. Lack of source material was a recurring problem confirming our absence from official history and the need for us to document our past and preserve our culture. In recognition of these heavy obligations and with our own insecurity about writing, that first chapter took on a very lofty tone. We were the official translators, making politically coherent what were disparate and uncommitted experiences. However, after we had toiled over several drafts and redrafts, we were forced to reconsider that quasi-academic approach, as we gradually came to realize that this was contradictory. If this first statement was to speak directly of and to our experiences, how could we adopt the uneasy, uncomfortable tone of a small group of academics? Were our lives to be primarily realized through research?

Abandoning that stance made the unstated decision clearer. The book had to be accessible, so that it would reach as many women as possible. Not all women had been active and new generations were coming up who knew nothing of the struggles their sisters had waged. We had, therefore, to bypass all those who would come with expectations of intellectual niceties. We were not denying the value of research but we had to be clear that a book grounded in experience, that was evolving as collective autobiography, had to be written in a clear and unambiguous style.

We take up our story in Africa, six thousand years after the Ancient Egyptians first began to establish Africa's creativity and genius in the world, and shortly before the Europeans first set foot on African soil for the purpose of plunder. By this time, our African ancestors had established a variety of cultures and societies, using whatever different means of production were available to them. We were living as nomads, as hunters and gatherers, as members of settled farming communities and as residents of flourishing trading towns and cities. We were living in feudal societies, paying taxes to local chiefs and rulers; in slave societies, where power, class and privilege were already strictly established; and in communal societies, where resources and decision-making were shared, often on a matriarchal basis. Above all, we were living in societies which we ourselves had determined.

So Europe's first contact with the land of our ancestors had one purpose — to extract as much as it could. And Europeans were in a position to take the offensive. They had already learnt about the potential of gunpowder from the Chinese, and internal wars had ensured that they had a highly-developed

knowledge of guns and cannons. Using force and other dubious forms of persuasion, they set about exchanging their second-hand clothing, household utensils and guns for what later proved to be among Africa's most prized resources — gold for much-needed coinage, minerals such as iron, and precious substances like ivory. But this exploitative relationship was only the beginning. Africa would pay an even greater price in years to come, in the form of her most precious resource of all — us, her people.

It would have been easy if that kind of decision about style meant that we went ahead and wrote the rest of the book. Situations kept arising which called for responses from the whole Black community, and this put us under a lot more pressure. In 1981, for example, there was the need to mobilize the community in the wake of the New Cross Massacre, and some of us were involved in organizing the demonstration. Later that year, some of the women in the collective were involved in the Defence Campaigns that became necessary after the Brixton uprisings, taking on leading roles within them. At the same time we were busy organizing the other Black women, not only in our local Black women's groups but also in OWAAD. So there were constant meetings to attend, conferences to organize (such as health and education) and a lot of campaigning to be done. All this was at a time when our community had no GLC funding to rely on, no full-time political workers and no established premises. In other words, everything we did was in our own time, during the evenings and at weekends. It had to be fitted around the demands of our paid work, and our family commitments. So it was hardly surprising that the original group of women who were involved in the book project dwindled, and despite repeated calls for others to get involved it proved impossible to recruit new members. By now, two of the three of us had three young children and as we moved from high activity to questioning and introspection we sometimes wondered if it was worth proceeding and if the time for celebrating Black women's struggles was passing.

These pressures on us from personal and political realities were important because they informed the writing and our relationship with the other participants, the interviewees. Our experiences of trying to combine so many different aspects of our lives simply underscored the points the book was making about what Black women were going through and surviving. The struggles to fit in everything, to ride a disappointment, cancel a meeting, find work space, snatch a page of work time while children slept and still keep optimistic, meant that we were all sharing the same reality. As we continued to write and got deeper into the book and the interviews, this fusion became stronger. It became increasingly apparent that we were speaking from one large and common well of experience. This is something that we all know theoretically or even instinctively but in writing we had approached the task of interviewing research. We had hundreds of questions to ask every conceivable type of Black woman but as we abandoned the earliest draft of the first chapter, we threw out our detailed questionnaires. Instead we met women and we talked with them and taped the conversations. They, in turn, suggested other people we should interview until in the end we spoke to nearly a hundred women. Sharing experiences with so many women, we quickly found the links and echoes of our own lives. Recognition made for a common bond: yes, this was what happened between me and my mother . . . yes, that was my school too . . . yes, there's always one of them to show you . . . I felt like that too . . . yes . . . yes . . .

Our experience of Britain has often served to compound this notion that whiteness and success are synonymous, leading us to a confused sense of self and culture. Although our mothers have been instrumental in perpetuating our culture through us, the experience of living here made some of them seek out ways of protecting us from racism, by encouraging us to assume the trappings of the dominant culture, or to "act white". But we have invariably learnt that the best way to protect ourselves from racism is to equip ourselves with our culture, and use it as a buffer against the society's assaults on our identity.

My parents, although both Black, were from very different backgrounds. My father was Nigerian and my mother Jamaican. Even now their marriage can be difficult but at the time it was disastrous. They faced opposition on all sides. My father's family accused him of going to Britain and marrying the descendant of slaves. My mother's family didn't want anything to do with her marrying a Black African. She had "spoiled" herself. It was all to do with status. A beautiful brown-skin girl wasted.

With that kind of confused, culturally insecure background it was understandable that I took on white ways. My father schooled me to "speak properly" so I sounded white because he was keen on education so even when looking at my Black face, people used to ask if I was mixed because of my accent. I did come over to others, especially other Black girls, as though I was trying to act white. They felt that I was just being snobbish. The white girls tolerated me. When they made their racist comments, it was a case of "Not you, you're different". That was what I had to live with.

Fortunately, it didn't last and as I came through my mid-teens I did begin to change. From there I made a conscious effort to take on my mother's culture. Why my mother's? Only with Black Power did Africa become fashionable. Before that, when I was just into an understanding, I thought that to be accepted meant to be West Indian. So I taught myself to speak Jamaican and learnt how to cook — not as a programme, but I'd go to the kitchen and watch my mother. I'd go and watch a domino match, go to a shabeen, picking up bits of Black life all the time. It was the only way I could learn to feel part of my people.

When I sent my daughter to school, I can remember her coming home one day and asking me why God had made her Black. That really hurt me. I asked her if she didn't like being Black, and she said no, she didn't because she was the only Black child in her school. I told her God chose to make some of us Black and some of us white, and there's no difference between us. But still she didn't want me to plait her hair, I had to put it in a pony-tail all the time, otherwise she would cry, because all the other kids had their hair flowing down . . . That made me aware that there was a lot of prejudice in the schools that was affecting the kids deeply.

They never encouraged you or asked you what you would like to do when you leave school. I had always been made to feel that because I was Black, I was stupid and not good enough for much. You got that impression from TV as well — that we were just maids, butlers, servants in fact. My Careers Officer tried to send me to a factory interview. It was the best they felt they could do for someone with no O levels. But I didn't turn up for the interview. Although I wasn't qualified, I didn't want a factory job.

As our stories merged we became less the objective recorders and translators of experience and more clearly one of the voices. These were voices that we could now trust. The "we" became stronger, paramount — conscious and unequivocal. It was the guiding force in a seamless stream of shared experiences from grandmothers, mothers, aunts and sisters.

It was to alleviate these miseries that we first began to look for a collective means to make life more bearable. Women figure strongly in the initial and predominantly informal efforts we made to establish our communities and maintain ourselves. The hairdressing salon, for example, served many Black women as a meeting place and more often than not the "salon" would be based in somebody's front parlour, since no European hairstylist would cater for our particular needs. Going along to have your hair pressed or relaxed was a social event, an opportunity to meet and exchange stories with other women. And the woman who was the best source of information was, of course, the hairdresser who was well-placed to give advice, support and reassurance to others. Most significantly, we organized the "Pardner" system through which we saved regularly and collectively. By withdrawing the money we pooled on a rota basis, we gave ourselves access to much-needed funds.

It was mainly women who set up the pardners. Nine out of ten of the pardners schemes had a woman in charge of them. It was done on a village or family basis. Whoever's needs were greater, they got the deposit on a house. It was the woman who held on to the money and paid down the deposit, but still no home could be put in her name. Later people started to have selling parties. It helped to pay the mortgage, but it also provided us with somewhere to go. That's why they started.

The Pardner system has survived up to the present day as a widely-used and efficient community money-lending and saving scheme. But in those early days, it provided us with the only regular and available source of funds when a lump sum was needed as a down-payment on a mortgage or to cover the cost of our children's air tickets. In the absence of friendly building societies or sympathetic bank managers, self-reliance was a common objective and served to bind us together as we strove to establish our communities.

Through our embryonic churches, too, we gave the help and support to new immigrants which the British government and people had failed to offer. The churches provided Black women with one of our main sources of support and sustenance, offering some continuity with the forms of social and community organizations we had known in the Caribbean. For many of us, these churches offered the only form of recreation we had to relieve the pressures of our working lives, and to support an otherwise bleak existence.

This confirmation of the importance of the testimonies meant that we relied more and more on them to structure the frame of the book. It was not just a case of writing an analysis or using the interviews as illustration; one process informed the other. We acknowledged that beyond the small group of people who sat down and wrote, there was a larger collective of contributors to be consulted and sometimes to advise on what was to go in. In this, the gathering together of writers that had earlier defeated us became a little more real.

The collective writing experience of *The Heart of the Race* was a significant learning process for all of us who were involved. We discovered something not only about the possibilities of writing but also about what working together really meant in the most direct and personal of ways. In the end, it kept us and the project together for four years. This is what has surprised many people because we could find ways of fusing three sets of ideas and styles and still work together. We also found that collective writing increases one's sense of responsibility and accountability because if we felt like giving up, we had to stop to consider the other people involved. Once the project seemed real and the goals possible, we were committed and could not let each other down.

We should make it clear, however, that in recounting our experiences we are not prescribing for others — we do not expect other Black women to repeat them in any direct way. We needed to write in this way because the nature of the project demanded many voices contributing in different ways. We ourselves may not necessarily continue writing in this way in future. Nor do we see ourselves as a permanent group. But in showing how the collective process works we hope that we have shown a different approach to writing and perhaps may encourage other writers who might wish to work together. Perhaps more Black women will begin to articulate some of their experiences, knowing that whatever the commitments, preoccupations or constraints, we can write. We must do this; in order for our presence here to become more visible we must set down what we have done. We must consider our gains, examine, honestly, some of the contradictions within our community and make links with our sisters about what has to be done. We have to do these things in every possible way.

LAURETTA NGCOBO

Lauretta Ngcobo was born Gwina in South Africa. After the 1960 political upheavals there, she left the country and went into exile with three of her children, living in various parts of Africa before settling in Great Britain fifteen years ago. Soon after arriving in England, she wrote her first published novel, *Cross of Gold* (Longman Drumbeat, 1981), based on life among black people in South Africa. She works full-time as a teacher at an infants' school in London and is also a part-time tutor in Black Women's Literature in the Extra-Mural Department of London University. She is currently writing a novel about South African black women and their life and struggle in the rural areas.

* * *

MY LIFE AND MY WRITING

I am an exiled South African and, although I have lived in several parts of the world for the past twenty-odd years, I remain an exiled South African. The fact of exile in itself, the reluctant choice to live away from one's country of birth, impels me to remain, in my heart of hearts, none other than a South African. I think South African, I feel South African and I write South African. Therefore, on the British scene, I remain an immigrant writer. My only qualification as a Black British writer is that Britain gave me my expression, where South Africa, by her repressive nature, had muzzled me. I value the privilege to write what I feel and think. So Britain has a special place in my craft, a prized place — she gave me what South Africa, my country, could not give me. In this sense I am a British writer — no other country afforded me this.

I don't think I know why I write, I just know I must. I scribble a lot that I know will never be read by anyone, for since I was a little girl by conditioning, I never expected anyone to read anything that I wrote, outside my classroom assignments. I feel the need to communicate with myself. It is a duty to myself. Yet, by its very nature, writing is an outgoing channel of communication, no matter how private. The fact that my innermost thoughts are expressed means that I have no longer any control over them — they are out, even if I should lock them up in some cupboard. From that time on, no matter how unconsciously, I also live in the hope that someone, sometime, will stumble over them and share them with me. So perhaps there is no such thing as writing for oneself. Apart from clarifying one's own thinking, writing is an act of service to one's own community, whether one writes joyously to celebrate communal achievements or to share personal joys and sorrows or to offer insights into the complexities of life. Writing draws one out from the private world and focuses the public eye, not only on what is being said but on the writer as well. This makes it clear that for me, as long as I remained in South Africa, writing was a minefield of contradictions. If by writing one is in communication with the rest of one's society, it stands to reason that I was up against that society that I wished to serve, for the watertight barriers of apartheid South Africa cannot be penetrated through writing.

Picking up a Black paper in the days before I left South Africa, one was aware of the practised art of hedging and frivolity on the part of the reporters — they reported every crime at every street corner, every family's sordid quarrel, and the rest was sport. Our society was muzzled breathless. There was a relentless persecution of those writers and journalists who dared speak the truth. In their reports of the self-mutilating ghettos, they exposed what the system was doing to destroy the lives of men and women. The government launched a witch-hunt against all so-called agitators — and there are no better agitators than those who wield the pen. Most of those writers and journalists were finally forced to leave the country and face exile. So was I — not so much for writing, but for political reasons.

Today, the new generation of South African writers are more

daring, for they seem more prepared to pay the price. Their papers and their books are still being banned as ours were in the past. The writers themselves are banned and imprisoned, for to write one has to tread through a minefield of innumerable clauses of censorship. Under the Publications and Entertainments Acts of 1963, every subject is potent and out of bounds for the African writer. In the enforcement of this law and various clauses in other laws, South Africa boasts of at least ninety-seven possible infringements of the laws of censorship — things subversive, offensive, obscene and blasphemous; things that might bring ridicule or contempt against the inhabitants of South Africa; and, of course, things prejudicial to the safety of the State. And, for the Black South African, as though these were not enough, the government has moved over the years to establish organizations whose primary aim is to sift and select officially acceptable themes and writings from the unacceptable.

Above all else, the greatest limitation for the Black writer is the Bantu Education Act of 1953. It has had a great effect on the type of writer as well as on the standard of that writing, which, logically, is linked with the type of education one receives. Where the primary aim of education is deliberately and explicitly to control the direction and level of mental development, to suit the individual for a lower status in society, so will it affect the quality of the writer and the writing. Through its limitations on the African child, it has managed to cut every African off from the main stream of world literature which could otherwise act as a model and an inspiration. I have shared these limitations with all Black South Africans whether male or female.

When I was a child, no one made the effort to make me aware of the oppression of my people in South Africa. In the countryside, where people hold on desperately to their values, their pride as a people, they would not admit openly, especially to the children, that their whole life was demeaned. They went hungry, they went in rags, but as a child I accepted these as facts of life, like the grass being green and the rocks hard. My father died when I was very young and so did many of my friends' fathers that I knew — I accepted it as life, not as a consequence of a way of life. This inevitability about life remains one of the things I try to probe and refute when I can; it stocks my thinking and my writings, it fuels my anger and propels me to probe.

Life is a lie that comes parcelled in imperatives which need to be exposed for the banal reality they are. It is amazing how much these parcelled out inaccuracies determine our lives and undermine the truth. Blacks are inferior and unintelligent; so-called Third World countries are poor; men are more important, intelligent and fit for power than women. In my own life, the way I live in itself seeks to disprove these fallacies. Where some people write to inform, to prescribe or to entertain, I find that I often write to question, to probe. I pose questions even when I find it hard to answer them precisely because I find it hard to answer questions.

However, in addition to these constraints, an awareness is fettered in my consciousness that I have never been a fully participating member of my own society; that somehow I was born on and kept on the periphery of life. In my society, outside the all-dominating white man's world, there was yet another exclusive zone from which I was kept out and that was the larger world of African men. I learned to accept that there was no validity in what women thought and said. Men met regularly in places where women were not expected to attend and they discussed community issues to the exclusion of women. I have distinct memories of those weekly announcments — my grandfather's sombre Sunday voice inviting men to a meeting at some designated spot behind the dipping tank, where they met after dipping their cattle on Thursday mornings. It went without saying that no woman would be there. In a society with sharp divisions of work roles, women did not tend cattle and could not be at the dipping site on a Thursday morning at 10 a.m., when men "talked". I puzzled for many years why my grandfather, a very quiet man, could go and "talk", leaving behind my grandmother who did all the talking around the home and did it most incisively. Hers is the voice I remember most clearly from my youth. Yet she did not attend the Nkwali meetings!

Later, as a grown woman involved in the politics of protest and the struggle against apartheid, I slowly came to realize that mine was a cheering role, in support of the men. I had no voice; I could only concur and never contradict nor offer alternatives. In short, men had (and still have) the exclusive right to initiate ideas and were (are) provided with the forums of expression for those ideas. They are raised on a diet of confidence-builders and morale-boosters. All decision-making positions are still in the hands of men, in spite of the lessons of a rigorous political struggle.

This background has had a very direct bearing on my writing. I have often been asked why I speak through my male characters while my women are locked in suffocating silence. In my novel *Cross of Gold* (1981) the only woman who had it in her to strike out and explore alone without a man to lean on was Sindisiwe. But Sindisiwe dies in the first chapter of the book. My women are often alone, not dependent on any male, and they suffer without complaining. When I was first asked about these characters, it took my breath away. I had not realized it until then. This, of course, reflects my society in the rural areas of South Africa, where I grew up.

I was brought up almost exclusively by women. They were strong, independent and silent. As I have said, my father died young, like many Blackmen in South Africa; he was thirty-four. I was seven years old, and I missed him a lot — but I missed the idea of a father rather than the man himself, for I never really knew him. My mother tells of an incident that hurt him badly: on one of his homecomings he arrived on the same day as one of many uncles — and I ran excitedly to the wrong man. I remember about two or three short intimate moments between us which I have treasured through the years. The rest is a patchwork of memories, built from photographs and the many anecdotes that Mother fondly tells to this very day. The migrant labour system not only destroys family life, but it is harsh on our mothers. Faced with this universal deprivation, the women have no choice but to be strong in their silent endurance. I hope some day to write about their courage and decisiveness in the absence of men.

Since I was the daughter of such mothers, it was inescapable that I should turn out very much like them: fertile and rich from within but silent or barren from without. I was approaching fifty when my first book was published in London, and my next book has been struggling through for the last four years. Even after being published (and perhaps I now write to be published), I still find it hard to open out to the world. Yet for me there is an uninhibited euphoric experience when I do write. It is as if I was deaf before and can now hear; I was mute, now I can speak. When people come up to me and say, "I enjoyed your book", "I read your article", "I thought your speech was good", "I heard you on the radio" — each time I am liberated, for someone is listening; someone has taken time to hear me. When one white South African woman wrote what was my worst review, and later told me to my face what a hash of a job I had made in writing my book, I laughed to her face, for she was trying to force back the bars across my path of escape. She was too late. People were listening, the caged bird had flown and, all around the world, people could hear me.

In my writing I am aware of a force, a releasing power. It is a pleasurable force that none the less is not completely under my control. I am vaguely aware of another reality, another mysterious dimension of self which I long to tap and bring under the control of my familiar self — thus I write. I enjoy writing when I can. It arises from the depths I cannot reach. Sometimes it intrudes into my daily routine at very inconvenient times, or it awakens me in the middle of the night. Occasionally the intrusion lasts for days and it can be quite severe on my mind and my feelings and my working routine. If I am unable to comply with its dictates to sit down and express myself, as is often the case in my crowded life, then I am torn apart by the storm within. It is like a fever and I am impossible to live with for myself and for my family.

When I first started writing, it was always in obedience to this dominant self. It breaks through all my defences. There was no set pattern or logical sequence of one event following another. But, as I had never intended to write for publication, this was no problem. My gypsy spirit roamed freely over any subject of choice. In this way, a sense of indiscipline was established.

It is hard for me to impose a routine that carries me from incident to incident, from day to day. I can write furiously for days and days; more often it is nights and nights, going sleepless until I am ready to collapse, as long as the fugitive spirit lingers on. Then one day a silence descends on me. I stop writing and rationality seals it in — I cannot then write one page if left to myself. I still hold a full-time job as a teacher in an infants' school. Sometimes these two selves are warring, tearing me apart. There is no direct conflict as such, but I find I cannot clinically allocate my time between the day hours of logical simplicity and the night hours of flightful fancy. When they do overlap, I live in a daze. It follows also that I cannot keep to the sequence of events as strictly as many other writers do, for the memory of a place or event that opens the floodgates is not necessarily what the storyline orders.

So, often I spend hours pinning my episodes together at the seams. I cannot think of a more time-consuming way to write. I would not recommend it to any young writer who has the faintest rudiments of self-discipline. Even now I am struggling to bring my disordered literary self together.

There was a time when I could expend any amount of time, thought and emotion on writing because I had no time limit to my expression and no deadlines to meet. When I got published I had no idea that this roaming spirit was going to suffer threats. The publication of *Cross of Gold* changed all that. There was a new premium on my time. I was invited here and there; I was asked to write this and that. This came most unexpectedly. The range of topics I was asked to think and talk about was wide. I still wonder why people think I should know about or hold views on so many varied subjects. Things that were quite removed from my life and things that I had known of vaguely became challenging to me. I had to read a lot more widely. This factual diet does little for my creativity — especially considering how limited time is between my teaching job, my "factual" reading and speechifying and creativity. What I need as a writer, more than anything, is time. I wish I did not have to work; or better still, that I could write a best-seller and so not need my nine-to-five job. I have since wondered why writers have to make the choice, either to write and starve, or to work for a livelihood and not write.

Having talked so much about my experience as a South African-made writer, I feel I ought to say one word about being a British writer. I have been in England for about fifteen years. On the other hand I lived in South Africa for about thirty-five years.

The quality of these two phases of my life is both very deep and varied; one embraces childhood, the other is selective adult experience. I have not exhausted my South African experience — I do not know if I will exhaust this. Perhaps one day I'll write a book about Britain.

The impact of the British experience falls on a padded cushion and often I am aware that this experience is not as raw for me as for many of my people here — nothing in the world can be as devastating as South Africa, so the British experience seems mild by comparison. What I feel most acutely is that Britain is not my place. In spite of the length of my stay, I feel I am passing through, and that Britain's oppression of Black people is not mine to destroy; I have battles to fight elsewhere. Yet those who are born British or have embraced the Queendom have other responsibilities to themselves and to our communities here. I am with them in their fight, for I know better than most the kind of evil they are up against. They suffer the same compulsions that I do, as deep as the history of Black oppression; they have the same duty as I have — the duty to be free.

I have already indicated that whether I am in South Africa or Britain I suffer mainly on account of my colour and my sex. The most instinctive reaction to all this is to cry out: "Burn the structures down!" But this is easier said than done. A political structure such as South African apartheid or the British brand of racism is easier to burn down than a social structure such as male domination. How does one free the woman without burning the whole society down?

Looking into the future, I wonder if it will prove to have been easier to fight the oppression of apartheid than it will ever be to set women free in our societies. Writing in the mid-1980s and watching the Black neighbourhoods burning in South Africa and our people dying in large numbers, I know this is a very serious assertion I am making. Male domination does not "burn down". Like treating a cancer, we must burn the diseased tissues of society's thinking without killing off the live creature.

EXTRACT FROM *CROSS OF GOLD*

Until that day I had prided myself on my ability to organize my life. Now nothing mattered. I had no desire to order my life neatly; I did not care if I was late for work or not, or if I ever went to work again. The events of the previous day had marked the end of life as I had known it. That was another chapter. A new life was to begin, a new outlook, full of new fears. Even as I lay there, a new resolve was being born in me; something new and strange was fluttering deep down in my being which seemed to stir; and help me to stand alone.

What I felt was an upsurge from the pit of my life, something that I knew could never be plucked away from me; for this feeling was different. It was not a grafted idea from you or from the eloquent speeches of the past weeks and months. That cold bed, at that hazy time of dawn, was the cradle of something new in me, something that would order the chaos in my life and in the world around me; for how else could my life and our life be described? I had up till then accepted the order of my world as unchangeable and immovable as an act of God. But then a new conviction, as yet undefined, rose up in me like a pillar. Out of the void of my indifferent empty days had arisen this cold, concrete, solid feeling and only a feeling as cold and as strong as this could bridge forever the chasm and the darkness of the abyss of injustice that had become the climate of our South African life.

I began to know what it is that moved you and others like you to those feats of daring. I stirred to get up but a strange sensation like fear gripped me. I was afraid to wake up and face another day; I feared the shadow of the previous day. In that muted silence of dawn I recalled the silence that had followed the passionate crackle of bullets and the fumes of hate.

More out of force of habit than my own volition, I stepped out into the cold morning air. I was on my way to work at Mrs Potgieter's house. I would be forced to tell her my husband was "involved"; he was one of the "agitators". I did not care then if the whole world knew. I meant to confront Mrs Potgieter with a request from an equal, to go and see my husband in jail that afternoon. If she refused, I would terminate my services on the spot.

Old habits die hard. For one moment my newly acquired conviction faltered. I felt so exposed and alone in a literal sense, but I walked to my place of work though I felt guilty of some unknown betrayal. I did not care when I entered the gate twenty minutes late. I could not remember being even five minutes late before, so well ordered was my life. I had been so careful never to see the other side of my employer. This was in accordance with my life. I had even acquired the ability to live and work with the same woman, just the two of us and her child, everyday, and still run parallel. If you keep on the right side of your socio-legal side of the street, including never leaving your pass behind in another handbag, generally nothing drastic will happen to you. And because order came to me without effort, I did not find it difficult to keep on the safe side of the line at a safe distance, keeping my life well regulated like a clock.

But the shootings of the previous day had changed all that, and would change much more. To begin with, I stayed away for three days, because those days were observed for national mourning. I went back on the fourth day expecting the sack but I was surprised to find Mrs Potgieter sullen but ready to let me continue. The next few days were a maze in which I lost myself — days at work in the mornings, visits to jail in the afternoons, visits to the hospitals in the evenings and half-nights at the "tebelong" where we sang solemn songs and listened to vague speeches that ominously hinted at the reversal of positions, when losers would become the winners.

Mrs Potgieter's sullen mood persisted. Never having been cheerful at the best of times, she grew suspicious and filled the whole air with ominous impatience. The break had to come. Mrs Potgieter became very critical and saw to it that none of her criticisms left me even an illusion of self-respect. Where previously she had merely pointed out mistakes, she now made a point not only of correcting the mistake but of making some reference to my husband, "who wants to rule the country — rule white people!"

Until then I had drifted about the workplace like a shadow, a mere mechanical, impersonal creature, obeying orders with apathetic resignation. From then on they could no longer ignore me for I had suddenly solidified into a real person and by my very presence I formed a climate of opinion in that household. I was no longer prepared to suffer the torment of pretence. How could I avoid being myself; living side by side with my body?

I was no longer the same Sindisiwe she had known before; I had been tossed in the great upsurge that had rocked the country, and like many other people I was waking up to a new life. And pink people, as usual, were blind to these eloquent changes.

You see, things had "settled" with surprising rapidity, at least on the outside. People went about their daily chores as before, and they still smiled and sang more than they wept. But this was only the scab that covered the wound that could never heal again. We worked, talked, smiled and sang because we had a new school that met in darkness and taught us to believe in ourselves — a belief that sprang out of the ruins; a school in the ability to attain freedom and above all a school in avenging all the wrongs against all our people. We were determined to learn our lesson well, and pass it on to those around us and to our children. No longer for us was the stoic quality of acceptance of our lot. My new self showed through me; it quivered in my voice that strained my self-control every time I spoke to her; it stood out in me, steady, upright and strong, redirecting and compelling, I could no longer be ignored.

On the other hand, Mrs Potgieter's irritation was growing visible and provocative. I knew the end was near; I would never again obey orders with apathetic resignation. One day, she dressed herself most beautifully in preparation for some unknown occasion. And more as an order than a request, in her most deliberately assertive voice, she told me that I would have to remain with her daughter for the afternoon and the evening of that day and from then on I would have to stay late three days of every week, because she had recently joined some club.

I did not wait for any further instructions — in the briefest answer I told her that she would have to give those instructions to someone else. I said it with no more show of feeling than a slight quiver in the voice, and I did not answer another word to the torrent of scalding words that followed.

BIBLIOGRAPHY

AMRYL JOHNSON

Sequins for a Ragged Hem, Virago, 1988.
Long Road to Nowhere, Virago, 1985.
Her work also appears in the following anthologies:
News For Babylon (ed. James Berry), Chatto & Windus, 1984.
Facing the Sea (ed. Anne Walmsley and Nick Caister), Heinemann, 1986.
With a Poet's Eye, Tate Gallery Publications, 1986.
Watchers and Seekers (ed. Rhonda Cobham and Merle Collins), The Women's Press, 1987.

MAUD SULTER

As a Blackwoman, Akira Press, 1985.
Her work also appears in:
'Wild Women Don't Get the Blues: Alice Walker in conversation with Maud Sulter' in *Charting the Journey: Writings by Black and Third World Women* (eds. Shabnan Grewal *et. al.*), Sheba, 1988;
'Everywoman's Right, Nobody's Victory' in *Through the Break* (eds. Pearlie McNeill *et. al.*) Sheba, 1987.

AGNES SAM

"What Passing Bell" (Prologue), *Kunapipi*, Vol. IV, No. 1, Dangaroo Press, Denmark, 1982.
"Poppy", *Kunapipi*, Vol. VI, No. 1, Dangaroo Press, Denmark, 1985.
"The Seed", *Kunapipi*, Vol. VII, No. 1, Dangaroo Press, Denmark, 1985 and in *Charting the Journey* (eds. Shabnam Grewal *et. al.*) Sheba, 1988.
"The Dove", *The Story Must Be Told*, Konigshausen and Neumann, West Germany, 1986; also published in *A Double Colonization*, Dangaroo Press, Denmark, 1986.
"South Africa: Guest of Honour Amongst the Uninvited Newcomers

to England's Great Tradition", *A Double Colonization*, Dangaroo Press, Denmark, 1986.

"A Tribute to Bessie Head", *Women's Review*, London, 1986; also published in *Kunapipi*, Vol. VIII, No. 1, Dangaroo Press, Denmark, 1986.

VALERIE BLOOM

Touch Mi; Tell Mi, Bogle L'Ouverture, 1983.

Her work also appears in the following anthologies:

News For Babylon (ed. James Berry), Chatto & Windus, 1984.

Penguin Book of Caribbean Verse in English (ed. Paula Burnett), Penguin, 1986.

A First, A Second, A Third and *A Fourth Poetry Books* (ed. John Foster), Oxford University Press, 1979, 1980, 1982, 1982.

Caribbean Poetry Now (ed. Stewart Brown), Hodder & Stoughton, 1986.

I Like That Stuff (ed. Morag Styles), Cambridge University Press, 1984.

You'll Love That Stuff (ed. Morag Styles), Cambridge University Press, 1987.

GRACE NICHOLS

i is a long memoried woman, Karnak House, 1983.

The Fat Black Woman's Poems, Virago, 1984.

Whole of a Morning Sky, Virago, 1986.

Trust You, Wriggly, Hodder & Stoughton, 1981.

Baby Fish and Other Stories, self-published, 1983.

Her work also appears in many poetry anthologies.

MARSHA PRESCOD

Land of Rope and Tory, Akira Press, 1985.

THE COLLECTIVE

The Heart of the Race: Black Women's Lives in Britain, Virago, 1985.

LAURETTA NGCOBO

Cross of Gold, Longman, 1981.